THE
MARVELOUS SAGA
OF THE
MERCANARY™

A SELLS-WORD'S NOVEL
OR SOMETHING

DAVID REYNOLDS

ISBN-13: 978-1-927996-08-9

Published by Problematic Press.

To purchase additional copies of this book, please visit: http://problematicpress.com

Cover design, interior art, photos, illustrations, and graphics by David Reynolds.

MERCANARY™, the MERCANARY™ logo, and the hat logo are trademarks of Problematic Press.

This story
is for
each of you
that
see it through
to
the end.

CONTENTS OF THE MERCANARY™

Through cloudy skies, a spot of sun
And no mistaking
There's a chill in the air.

Hi

I'm your narrator.

I'm that voice in your head.

Hello.

Thanks for having me.

I'm the voice that wasn't there a moment ago, but it sure is now.

Pay no mind to me.

I'm just here to tell you a story.

Just play along.

Now, it isn't *my* story.

It's not *your* story, either.

Together, we'll make it *our* story, but that's not the whole of it, is it?

No.

This is *Harry's* story, and I'm sure he wouldn't appreciate us gossiping like this, but here we go.

Yes. I know.

You thought this was *The Marvelous Saga of the MERCANARY*™.

You aren't wrong, but this is Harry's story first.

Bear with me here.

You'll see where we're going once we get there.

Prologue

"BOAT TOURS! TEN BUCKS!"

Dawn breaks, gulls caw, and a loose fog cools the morning air as Harry awakes in the grass beside the street, a pile of vomit for his pillow. At least it was his own. Some would joke that Harrison Stockton Bueller's had a good night out on the town, but he'd tell you it's not so funny.

Harry attempts to take in the situation, champing his dry mouth like a horse at a bit. He didn't get far from the club, only making it to that corner of Harbour Drive where everything seems new and out of place. His head pounds, but his stomach aches worse. It's empty. He's hungry.

There's a fence along the waterfront now. Harry shambles closer to take a piss on it. A car slows as it drives past, gawking. He couldn't care less.

The fence wasn't always there, but it is most definitely there now. Town's been booming, and that means it's time for some new wrought iron fences. It used to be you could look right out through the Narrows, unimpeded, across a speck of sea out to the horizon; now, you get to see the same but through vertical metal bars. It adds perspective.

Zipping up, Harry searches his pockets for anything – cash, coin, smokes, diazepam – but only finds lint, his lighter, and crumpled receipts.

There's little left he can do. Harry struggles to contemplate his existence as he shuffles down the street, head throbbing, belly aching. He doesn't get very far before he droops down to sit on the sidewalk. Flashbacks intrude on his thoughts, reminding him how he got here.

Rae's gone now. She'll have nothing more to do with him. Harry doesn't blame her. He's a bum, and she's got drive. He hasn't worked in months now, and the dole's finally run out. He was living in her tiny one-room, but that's no longer an option. What's he supposed to do now? Where's he supposed to go? Should he enlist? He'd rather not think about any of it.

It's still too soon to deal with life's problems. He musters up some energy and gets back on his feet. One foot in front of the other, he trudges on despite his lack of enthusiasm.

There's little traffic this early on a Sunday, with no office workers' hustle and bustle. Some tourists are out and about. A cruise ship's in town.

Walking further along the street, Harry sees the iconic Signal Hill poking out of the mists like a cheap postcard. He nears a gate in the fence. Nearby, a stool rests beside a small boat tour shack. He just wants to rest his arse. No one would mind; they aren't booking tours this early.

Small groups of tourists meander past him through the gate. He watches them. Sight-seers from the cruise ship loiter in the area, plotting their itineraries. Some are clearly couples while others seem to be travelling solo. Many look like retired folk to Harry, mostly saps and suckers. There must be a fine line between carefree and careless.

"Excuse me? Young man?" A foreign voice calls out to him, "Do you often see whales?"

"What?" he replies. Harry was distant. It took a second for him to adapt to social interaction. The woman before him wore a splendid fanny pack. It was at Harry's eye level. "What do you mean – sees whales?"

"On your boat tours – do you often see whales on the tour?" Harry can't place the accent – is it German? Swiss?

"Yeah, I guess there are all sorts of whales to see out there. That's why people pay to go on the tours, I s'pose." He's being saucy, but she has mistaken his attitude for Newfie charm. He eyes her fanny pack greedily.

"I see," she responds, "and how much for the tour is it – per person?"

"Wha–" Harry begins to respond, but a desperate scheme takes shape in his mind. "Uhh," he hesitates, "well, it's just ten bucks a head."

Harry's never been on one of these boat tours, so he has no idea how low he set the bar.

The tourist thinks she just hit upon a great deal. She immediately recruits her friends. This is better than he had expected, so he stands upon the stool and, as it wobbles beneath his feet, he cries out: "BOAT TOURS! TEN BUCKS!"

This attracts others, and Harry takes their cash, too. He is content to swindle them all, stuffing their money into his back pocket and prattling gibberish about whales, puffins, and icebergs. They gleefully listen to his lies and wait patiently for his initiative.

Harry's farce attracts more than a dozen marks. He scans the crowd, guessing he has over a hundred in cash, enough for him to eat something and get out of town. Maybe he could hitch to the mainland, to labour on an orchard or go planting trees.

Rallying the herd, he leads them along the dock. As he passes along the ships he points each one out to the pliant tourists.

"And this one's a coast guard ship of some

sort," he began to fumble his bluff as he neared the end of the line. He neglected his escape route. That cursed fence blocks his path to the city's streets. The vertical bars aren't fit for climbing, but he spots some stacked containers that might allow him to jump clear over this barrier. That means quite a fall on the other side. It might hurt, but who'd be fool enough to follow him? As he turns from his audience he barks his farewell: "That wraps up our budget boat tour. I hope you all enjoyed viewing the boats. Thank you! Come again!"

Just like that, he's on the scuff!

His herd is baffled.

Harry doesn't look back. He imagines they're not pleased with his idea of a boat tour. His body aches, but the thrill pushes him on, foolheartedly, toward the containers. Harry scrambles over them, losing little momentum before flinging himself over the fence.

Time seems to slow as Harry drifts over the top of the bars, stretching as he falls to the concrete, anticipating the impact.

He hits the sidewalk. Crumpling violently, he tries to roll with it. Shaken, he staggers and finds that his wild leap has knocked over the topmost container. His pursuers are foiled by the fence.

Harry laughs at his fortune as he trots across the

street, nearing an alleyway. He breathes deeply and takes in the graffiti. The colours are dazzling even in the shade. He doesn't notice the silhouette of two large figures at the end of the alley.

Harry's so pleased he begins to whistle. He even greets the two locals: "Cheers!"

He's only two steps past them when they grab him. It happens so fast. With just a few cracks he goes down.

They loot his spoils, but he somehow feels he's paid a sort of penance.

The two brutes move on quick after their hit on Harry. He supposes they're smarter than he is.

As he shifts in the alley's dirt he mutters aloud, "It's time I go to sea."

Concussed

Harry gets to his feet – too quickly, perhaps, because he's seeing stars. He rests against the painted wall with his right hand. The stars dwindle but a few glinting specks refuse to vanish. Then he recognizes this is real. Three coins lay on the ground. Abandoned as worthless by his attackers, Harry collects the two loonies and a toonie. This'll do, he thinks.

The morning sun has broken through the clouds only a shred, and it's enough to bring some small sense of cheer, however fleeting that may be. Harry staggers up to Water Street, sizing up the situation.

Downtown almost nevers sleeps. Traffic of all kinds ebbs and flows throughout the day, and the tide will soon be coming in – a tide of freshly frustrated tourists, too, today. Harry knows he shouldn't stick around, but he hardly knows what to do with himself. He's not fit, honestly.

Rae runs through his thoughts repeatedly and without restraint.

Raelyn.

Raelyn Poppy.

There's no other like her, Harry thinks.

He recalls the time she snatched his hat when they were drinking in the woods with the crew. Of course, you know that they were underage. This was before they really "started dating." She ran off into a secluded grove, inviting Harry to come after her. He did.

Mercanary appreciates such moments.

That memory is cut short when he recalls her screaming how much she hated him. That was just a month ago. It's as if the moment is present, the memory is so clear. He pushes it aside.

Harry pats himself down again out of habit, as if searching his inventory. A nearby cat howls in unrequited heat. He comes up nil.

Mercanary appreciates Deltron as Can-Con. And, Mercanary appreciates Can-Con as much as he appreciates misdirection.

He needs his things, so he's off to see Vince.

When he moved out of Rae's, he moved his stuff into the shed behind Bob's burger joint –

Barthes' Burgers and Belgian Waffles – but that's on the other side of town. It's his dad's franchise; that's just Bob's outlet here in town. It doesn't matter right now, though, because Harry needs his personal effects, which he left at Vince's before they all went out to drown Harry's sorrows.

> Mercanary appreciates how to make Barthes' burgers despite rarely watching Bob.

Turning east, he staggers down the sidewalk, passing storefronts, pubs, grub, and lodging, swaying left to right with each step. He winces. He's dizzy. Leaning against a mermaid, Harry pauses.

Downtown is littered with these mermaid statues. It's a tourism thing. Arts grants were awarded. That sort of thing. Each one is painted by a seperate artist, and so each bears a different façade. Some artist actually convinced the city to allow this topless mermaid to be part of the downtown exhibit. She's some brazen, but she's cute and this is art, so it's valid.

> Mercanary appreciates that this little mermaid speaks moistly to no one.

A faint mist drifts across the street and sidewalk, skirting around Harry's ankles, and that oh-so-typically tropeish shiver travels up his spine. He shakes it off, and plods on to Vince's loft.

A flock of seagulls pick at food scraps left in

the empty street. Harry approaches as they realize they're down to the last good morsel. Four begin to squawk aggressively, each starving, and they spread their wings, posturing. He understands.

Harry should have known to cross the street. Instead, he tries to squeeze past these gulls, and it only riles them up.

Just a step after passing by, they take flight, and Harry fears the inevitable shitstorm.

"Fuck off, gulls!" he cries, pitifully, fleeing flecks of the grossest grey and white.

A server stands in the doorway of Wiggly's Finn-Feather, smoking before her shift begins. She looks over upon hearing Harry.

Mercanary appreciates and applauds the efforts of all essential workers. Mercanary also advocates for the exploited and the exhausted, valuing barmherzigkeit über alles.

Sure enough, the shitstorm ensues.

"Nooooo!" Harry bolts for just a few steps, quickening to dodge the incoming fecal matter.

Like some sort of plague-infested, slimy napalm, the seagulls rain their defecation all across the ground. Splats sound in succession, yet Harry remains unspoiled.

"HAHA!" he laughs with defiance, reverting back to his stagger.

The server smiles at his buffoonery from a distance, then she begins her shift.

Mercanary appreciates the ten cent plague with far more admiration than Fredric Wertham could ever muster.

Harry picks up his pace.

He recalls when he met Rae. It was on the dancefloor. He wasn't supposed to be there. He had snuck in. Fake ID. It wasn't even a bar. This was a high school dance for the drama festival. Harry wasn't taking drama, but he forged a pass and in he went, just like a proper actor would.

Harry stumbles a step, tripping, not noticing the uneven cracks in the sidewalk.

She radiated glee, dancing with two girlfriends, when he saw her and their eyes met.

It was classic.

It was cheesy.

Whichever you prefer.

A moment passed, and they smiled in sync.

A minute later, they were dancing together, her friends nearby but forgotten.

A half an hour later, and they were entwined in each other's limbs, engulfed in the curtains of the stage, hidden, searching, discovering, and just feet away from 200 or so other students and maybe a dozen chaperones. Neutral Milk Hotel's "Ghost" was playing, thumping, pounding as they crossed this threshold.

Then Harry finds himself in Vince's building, standing at the door to his loft. Vince is chill and a little bit wild, so they get along well, ever since first-year in university. He knocks.

"Enter!" Vince calls from inside. Harry turns the latch and enters the loft. It's a nice place. "Harry! You live."

"It's true."

"Not bad. That was a hard night."

"Eh, b'y."

The shower's running, but Vince is wearing a towel tied around his waist, collecting notes scattered about from table to desk to countertop. "I had to bail," he says without remorse. This is how friends roll.

"It's alright, Vince."

"I had to."

> Mercanary fully endorses St. Vincent's sentiments on such matters.

After a second, Vince follows up, asking, "Where'd you go after?"

"Fuck. Don't get me started."

"Yeah?"

"Yeah."

"Good enough, man. Here," Vince says. Handing a mug to Harry, he pours in a shot of spiced rum. "Help yourself to some coffee. I only put it on 20 minutes ago. You look like you need it."

"Thanks. I do." Harry was grateful, but he added, "Mind if I make some toast?"

"Do it up!"

"Eh, b'y. Thanks."

Vincent Lee, PhD, is an English professor. Or is he still tenure-track? Anyway, he's been moving up, and he took that literally, swapping his old basement one-bedroom for this dope and trendy loft. The doctor hired a decorator, and he's since been getting laid. Like, the loft's brick walls are lined with bookshelves, record crates, and dozens of nostalgic mementos like G.I. Joes, Transformers, and the Ninja Turtles. It's exactly what you'd imagine for this sort of geek, but the arrangement, the design? *That* is impeccable. That's the decorator's touch. It goes beyond what his own aesthetic could muster. Whatever. It's working for him, if for no one else. He puts his papers aside on the desk by the bay window to flip through his records, which he keeps in hand-crafted oak crates.

Harry studied business. He thinks it hasn't

helped him much. He takes half a loaf from the breadbox, puts two slices in the toaster, sets the timer, grabs the organic peanut butter from the fridge, pulls a knife from the drawer, and retrieves his satchel from beside Vincent's couch.

"Any chance I can sneak in a quick shower?"

Vince straightens up, turns, and gives Harry a look.

The timer ticks.

"Like, next," Harry adds. "You know I meant next."

"Of course." Vince returns to his records. "Help yourself. You'll find everything you need in there."

"Eh, b'y."

Harry checks his bag. It's a habit. It holds his phone, laptop, both chargers, a notebook, some half-emptied pens, a knit toque, a thin hoodie, three condoms, and what's left of his shrooms.

With the state he's in, Harry's content enough knowing the contents are secure. He's also comforted by the fact that he earlier scored $4 in coin.

"A-HA!" Vince snatches up a record.

DING!

Harry returns to butter his toast. "Don't put on a-ha. I can't take it right now." He remembers the

S.S. Kyle stranded in Harbour Grace, and he pushes those thoughts aside.

Mercanary appreciates the unexpected difficulties of working from home.

"What?" Vince is momentarily perplexed, striding to the record player. "I merely meant 'Eureka!' It's not a-ha. No worries."

"Thank fuck."

"Dude. Lighten up."

"Nah."

"Shit. For real, ease up in front of Patti. Don't fuck this up for me today."

The shower shuts off, and a husky voice sings muffled through a towel.

"I'll be best kind," Harry promises, pulling his stool closer to the bar, crumbs falling to the countertop more than the floor. "Thanks for the assist. I appreciate it." He does.

Vince gives him a trusting nod as he enters the bathroom, the only room with any privacy in the spacious loft apartment. "And Then She Kissed Me" by The Crystals spins. If he's playing singles, then he's really trying to make a good impression on Patti here.

Besides the bathroom, you'd have to go up to the roof just for some space. That has its own perks, of course, but Harry doesn't care right now.

He's too bummed.

Vince returns, clutching his towel before he lets it drop near his bed to pull on his jeans. He stretches into a shirt, picks up Patti's clothes, and passes them into her before flipping the record. Then, he pulls up a stool across from Harry.

"Where'd you stay last night?"

"Oh, I was out all night." Harry doesn't look up from his toast. "It's all good."

"Where are you staying tonight?"

"I've got errands to run all day." While there's plenty Harry should be addressing, this is ultimately a lie. "I'll see some friends and find a couch to crash on."

"You know, I have a couch."

"Eh, b'y. I hear ya. It's much appreciated. I'll keep yours in mind."

Patti exits the bathroom, fully clothed, hair dripping. She towels the tips of her moist ringlets to keep from soaking through her Ramones tee and smiles at Vince. Then, she greets the two, "Hey."

"Patti, this is my friend Harry. He's just stopping by for breakfast and a shower. The water's off at his place this morning."

Harry bluffs a shrug to Patti.

"Harry, this is Patti. She rocks." Vince hardly

misses a beat with such a simple cover; the introduction acts as bookends. Harry's savvy enough to observe and learn, but he's not sure why Vince'd bother putting on any act.

Harry's homeless.

So what?

He's not particularly embarrassed about it. He's been couch-hopping the past month, moving on after a night, two at the most, but the couches have run out at this rate. There's only so much abuse of others' hospitality Harry can live with.

"Hi." Harry's response comes with a moment's delay. He's distracted.

"It's thrown off his whole morning," Vince maintains, adding, "but the coffee's fresh... fresh-ish. It's kind of fresh. Okay. It's okay coffee. The coffee is okay."

"Yes, Dr. Seuss," Patti jests, and she pokes at Vince's ribs as she passes him by to grab a mug.

"There was no Seussian rhythm there." Vince couldn't let it slide; it's his field of expertise.

"Is that right?" Patti's not thrown off; she'll go toe-to-toe with anyone she damn well pleases, especially when she knows she's wrong. Still, this is when Harry excuses himself.

Patti and Vince flirt-fight while Harry showers. The pressure is weak but it's enough to wash the grime from his skin. No scrub could hope to cleanse his mind right now, though. Things are dark.

The water pours over his head, cold, filling his ears uncomfortably. He doesn't fuss. He lets it happen.

First, his thoughts drift back to memories of childhood swimming lessons. He never learned to swim. He'd always sink. Anyway, he failed and struggled and quit. It's not an encouraging thought.

Then, he reflects on how his friends used to crush, burn, or microwave their G.I. Joes. He'd never do anything like that. No. Instead, Harry would drown his G.I. Joes. It was only make-believe. In reality, he was only giving the Joes a bath, cleaning them off. It's not like they were ever destroyed. They were too precious to him to even consider it. How could his friends do that to their toys? Harry knew his Joes had more stories to tell.

He shuts off the water, dries himself, re-dresses, and returns to the others. They're examining album inserts and semi-entwined on the couch.

"I'm out."

"You're good?"

"As good as can be expected." Harry grabs his jacket and satchel.

"I guess."

"Thanks for everything, Vince." He puts on his Chucks.

"Any time."

"Nice meeting you, Patti." He opens the door.

"Same."

"You'll be alright?"

"Something like that." And Harry exits.

With nowhere to go and nothing to do, he wanders around downtown. Killing time, he heads up Duckworth and New Gower, then down Water, only to walk back along Harbour Drive. It's like he's baiting this morning's marks, but no one confronts him.

Eventually, he finds himself along Signal Hill's hiking trail. No one bothers him. He takes in a view of the harbour and the port. The fog is much thicker now. Harry catches a fleeting glimpse of a rainbow in the mist. It was crossing the twin peaks of the Narrows, from Fort Amherst to Signal Hill. It's there, and then it's gone, swallowed by the fog.

He keeps going – down into where there's more alders and clusters of evergreen trees – and finds a little grove, one with a makeshift firepit. All the trash littering the area is sun-bleached, so it seems no one's used it recently. He sits on a rock that was meant for sitting and opens his bag.

He should've begged Vince for a pack of

smokes. Fuck. That was a mistake. Hindsight tends to provide clairty, eh? Harry's settled on setting up camp here for the night. No smokes, though. That's going to hurt. He eyes his stash of shrooms.

Good enough.

He dumps the bag into his hand and swallows the lot as one mouthful.

It's sustenance, I s'pose, or coping. I don't judge, either way.

Mercanary appreciates the curious as well as the daring.

He opens his laptop, hits power, and it does nothing.

"What th– ?"

He closes it, opens it, hits power, and nothing.

"Motherfucker!"

This isn't going well.

Harry can't recall if the battery is charged or not. It's not like he can charge it out here, regardless, and he puts it back, pissed.

Taking a breath, he begins snapping off tree limbs. He needs some kindling, some firewood. It just happens to coincide well with blowing off a little steam.

It doesn't help that all the wood is damp, though.

Mercanary appreciates precarity as well as impermanence.

By the time Harry gets the kindling to set the branches ablaze, the shrooms have kicked in.

Like, fully.

He hadn't noticed. He was too focused on his task. He was still desperate and pissy. None of this is good.

Upon lighting the fire, Harry stands much too quickly.

R e a l i t y   s h i f t   s .

Cartoons emerge from the foliage.

Troubling cartoons, however.

Robots.

Pink robots.

Vicious pink robots surround his campsite.

One of the pink robots is an elephant with big, dopey ears that act as its wings. It climbs and swoops and dives, buzzing Harry in passing.

He clutches his bag for comfort.

There is no comfort.

Everyone's a robot.

Rae's a robot.

Harry's a robot, too.

Mercanary appreciates the challenge yet knows that one can free one's self.

The pink robots all have vapes. They mock Harry until he vapes, too. He does.

What is this?

"What is this?" Harry asks aloud.

I can't say for sure.

"I can't say for sure, but I shouldn't have a vape with me. I hate vapes," Harry recalls correctly.

His wits flicker in and out, but he throws down the stick he'd been holding, and occasionally chewing, only to discover that he's shivering. Severely. All that vaping was his breath. It's freezing here, even in summer some nights. The fire's almost out, too.

"F-f-f-f-f-f-f-f-f-f-f-c-k-c-k-c-k-c-k-c-k," he slurs through chittering teeth.

Sobering slightly, he adds more sticks from his stack, and stirs the fire's embers.

Everything is wavy and cel-shaded.

He shivers into his satchel, scrambling into his toque and hoodie. The extra layer doesn't help much.

He prods the embers until they flicker to flames.

Warmth returns, and Harry begins to relax a little, but despair overwhelms him. He wails. He bawls. He cries. He looks up to the night sky and, through the shifting fog and the parting clouds, the moon is a lemon meringue pie that is self-serving slices to the world via moonbeams. His heart breaks, and he weeps.

Then, he sleeps.

Sleeping doesn't bring the sort of peace one might desire. Harry suffers from nightmares at the best of times, and this is not the best of times.

He's a child.

In the forest.

It's dark and damp and cold and threatening.

A perverse presence clutches him from behind. It leans over his shoulder, grasping Harry's waist. A grotesque tongue lolls about Harry's earlobe, licking and slimy.

Harry screams into the night.

He doesn't wake, though.

This is his normal.

Waking the next morning, it's early. It's far too early for Harry's tastes. Sleeping under the stars often leads to rising at daybreak. It is what it is. Harry knows that, but he could use a day off from all these days off.

Still, he didn't freeze to death, so he heads back to town.

The clouds this morning are thick, heavy, waiting.

Harry's thoughts are as close to empty as humanly possible. Zen masters and new age gurus would envy the level of emptiness Harry's achieved in this moment, if only it weren't useless. There's nothing life-affirming in Harry's sense of nihilism this morning.

He finds himself downtown once again.

He has nothing on his mind, and he walks right past the monument to Terry Fox without any acknowledgment.

He walks across the beach rocks along the small shore and into the water. He's up to his knees.

The clouds seem to bear a storm within them. There's a distant crack and rumble. Harry's ears twitch, but he fails to really notice.

He's already up over his waist.

The sky darkens.

Mercanary – the half-bird, half-merman – appears on the beach, and, from there, he caws, "CHIRP, CHIRP! COO, COO!"

Harry takes a step further and then another step.

Mercanary draws a pair of machine guns from the emptiness behind his back. He fires volleys into the air.

RA-TA-TA-TA-TA-TATATATATATAH!

Harry turns, seeing Mercanary – the half-myth himself, full-bodied, in feathers and scales and glory – for the first time. He's captivated, but he remains up to his armpits in St. John's' harbour, which is not pleasant in any sense.

Mercanary slithers across the rocks and into the sea.

A figure takes shape in the ever-darkening storm clouds. It's like a sphynx but the head's more grotesque, trollish, with saucer-eyes that droop with gloom.

Mercanary leaps forth swimmingly just as Harry sees this Troll-Cat, too, when – FLASH/BANG! "CHIRP?" "What!?" – lightning crackles forth from this vile thing's cloudy maw!

The bolt strikes the salt water between Harry and the mercanary, blasting them apart.

Harry loses consciousness.

When his eyes open, he sees a clear sky and the smiling beak of a giant yellow canary. Brilliant, bold eyes beam into his own.

He jolts upright.

He's startled.

Makes sense.

I mean, this shit is weird.

Now, sitting on the beach, about two feet back from this beast-thing, Harry notices the scaly mer-tail.

"WHAT THE FUCK?"

"COO!"

"WHAT?"

"COO! COO! Chirp."

"Holy shit."

MERCANARY

A ZINE OF POETRY AND ADVENTURE

Famished

"Chirp, chirp."

"I know, I know," Harry replies. He's no longer soaked from head to toe, and he's sitting upright alongside this beast-thing.

"Coo, coo. Coo?"

"I don't know," Harry responds. "I just felt lost and empty. I dunno. I guess I ran out of ideas. I didn't know what else to do with myself. You know?"

"Chirp."

"Yeah." Harry's head sinks downward for a moment, but then he returns his gaze to this fantastic creature. "Who are you?"

"CHIRP!"

"Mercanary? Of course. Why not, right? I mean, the machine guns and all." He pauses, sizing up the mercanary mercenary named Mercanary, and then continues, "Where are your guns gone to?"

"COO!"

"Oh. Right. Naturally. Your invisible interdimensional holsters of holding. That's where they've disappeared to. Gotcha."

"CHIRP! CHIRP!"

"Well, it's about as plausible as a half-bird/half-merman. Where are you from?"

"Coo, coo, chirp, chirp, chirp!"

"WOW! That's insane!"

"Coo."

"Who owns you, sure?"

"CHIRP!"

"No way!"

"Chirp."

"Fuck. That's messed up. Like, we're bound?"

"Chirp, chirp."

"Okay. What're y'at here, anyways?"

"CHIRP, CHIRP! COO!"

"What the fuck? I don't need saving."

"Coo."

"I'll be fine."

"Coo, coo!"

"Whatever. That was a one-off. And I didn't go through with it. I'll be alright on my own."

"COO!"

"Whatever you say, buddy," Harry relents. "C'mon, we goes."

Harry picks himself up with a grunt while Mercanary bolts upright enthusiastically, beak agape and resembling the most charitable smile.

It's already past noon, the storm clouds are nowhere in sight, and the sun's been out long enough to dry out Harry's clothes. He reeks, though, as only St. John's Harbour can.

Harry and Mercanary walk through Harbourside Park toward the street.

"Where are we going to go?"

"Chirp, chirp!"

"All I do is walk around. Really? That's it?"

"CHIRP!"

"Have patience and just keep moving, yeah?"

"CHIRP! CHIRP!"

"Alright! Alright! Calm down, b'y."

Aimlessly, they walk up past the Four Sisters

and then head southwest down Duckworth. Thoughts race through Harry's mind. They're not about Rae; he's perplexed by this mercanary.

"How can you pull a trigger with those massive wings?" Harry asks Mercanary as they continue down the sidewalk. Passersby react with wrinkled eyebrows and disgusted looks. Harry doesn't notice.

"Chirp, chirp. Coo. Chirp!"

"Oh! I get it. Cool. That's a neat trick."

"CHIRP!"

"Can you even breathe underwater without gills?"

"Chirp!"

"Naturally. It doesn't matter," Harry responds, reflecting briefly on the logic of it all. "Have you heard that Great Big C song about the mermaid?"

"Coo."

"Yeah. I didn't think so."

"Coo, coo."

"Right. They wouldn't have those there."

Of course they wouldn't? Why would they?

The two haven't gone far down Duckworth when Harry asks aloud, "Are we there yet?"

They stop in front of a bookstore, the House of

Broken Books. A young woman wearing an "Enjoy Cock" tee, ripped jeans, and Docs finishes wrapping tape around a fresh poster, securing it to the light pole beside the entrance.

Mercanary appreciates that Björk was choosing her plague outfits 20 years in advance.

She smiles at Harry before grimacing, then she's quick to move along, posters tucked under her arm, carrying the tape applicator in one hand and covering her nose with the other. He smiles back, but she may have turned before noticing.

"Chirp!"

"Why are we here?"

"COO!"

"HA! That's a bold response. I wasn't being philosophical," Harry chides Mercanary, looking past him and scanning the ads glued to the pole behind this wonder. "What's this?"

"Chirp."

He traces the poster's exposition with his hand, reading the details.

"Dude! This is about 'zines!"

"CHIRP!"

"I know, right? I haven't seen anyone making 'zines in town since I was a kid. This is neat. It's a 'zine-making workshop."

"Chirp, chirp, chirp!"

"What? No. What would I even put in a 'zine?"

"Chirp, chirp!"

"But I haven't written any in years."

"CHIRP!"

"I guess," he responds to the beast. "Let me think about it." He goes to step away, then turns back to Mercanary and continues, "Listen. I need to change out of these clothes. Wanna come to Bob's?"

"Chirp!"

"Wicked. He's up on Torbay Road. It'll take us some time to get there, walking from here. Let's go."

Much of their journey passes in silence. The little they converse allows Mercanary to ask about Rae, but Harry's in no mood to go into details. He's resistant, and Mercanary doesn't push him too hard.

Mercanary appreciates existential dread as comedic relief.

So, of course, Harry's thoughts flutter between Rae and Mercanary until they reach the corner of Newfoundland and Torbay, the location of Bob's Barthes' Burgers and Belgian Waffles.

"This is it."

"Chirp!"

"Yeah. Their waffles are dope, dude. I'll check with Bob if I can put in a couple of hours in the dishpit for a combo."

They cross the half-filled parking lot of the shopping plaza and enter Bob's burger joint. A bell above the door signals their entrance. Staff quickly take in the new arrival, and upon seeing Harry there, they are relieved, returning to serving without a skip.

The woman behind the counter turns and calls out, "Harry! What brings you in today?"

"Nothing much. Where's Bob at?"

"Out. Gone to see a man about a horse or some shit."

"I hear ya." Harry knows exactly what Marg means, and he doesn't ask her to elaborate.

> Mercanary appreciates what often drives creativity.

"Anything I can do for ya?"

"Yeah, I just need to pick up some clothes. Can I get in the shed?"

"Just a minute. Lemme see to these few orders, and I'll take you out."

"Much appreciated, Marg. I can see you're busy. Take your time."

"I will."

She sniffs audibly, and then clutches her nose.

"Geezuz, 'Arry! Is that you?" Marg doesn't always drop her H's, but her bay accent comes through when she's flustered. She grew up in Lower Island Cove. Bob loves this about her. They aren't married, but they've been living common law for years.

"Sadly, yes."

"Lard t'underin'! Go on out be da door, and I'll bring y'upstairs. Take. A. Loooong. Shower."

"Thanks, Marg," Harry replies as he's already heading for the door. He had forgotten how much he stank, or he wouldn't have even entered the restaurant. Mercanary follows closely behind without causing a scene like Harry's stench.

Marg leads Harry to the upstairs apartment. It's modest enough, but Harry knows Bob's not hurting for funds. Not like he is, that's for sure. Harry's holding $4 in change, and that's it.

"You know where the shower's to, and there's a key on the rack for the shed. Grab whatever you need from your things. Don't touch the blue tarp."

"What's under the tarp?"

"Don't even ask, Harry," she gives him a look, and he knows. "There's leftovers in the fridge from last night. Help yourself."

"Thanks, Marg. You're too good to me. I'll put in a couple of hours for ya in the dishpit –"

She cuts him off, saying, "Honestly, I wouldn't even let Bob have you near the kitchen today, not with that stink that's on ya."

"Understandable." Harry gets it, but he still feels like shit. He'd rather earn a meal, but he's not about to argue with her generosity. "You're a real gem, Marg. Bob's a lucky fucker."

"That he is, me ducky!" And she leaves him to freshen and feed.

Mercanary swoops around the apartment, investigating knick-knacks and peeping out the windows. He spots Bob's records, and holds one up to show Harry. Harry nods, and Mercanary takes the vinyl from its sleeve, placing it on the turntable and dropping the needle into the groove to play "C.R.E.A.M." Mercanary bops.

> Mercanary appreciates that culture is created and that Wu-Tang is for the children.

Harry sighs. He takes his laptop from his satchel and plugs it in. It powers up, thankfully. He checks that it still works. It does. He's relieved and then shifts himself into the bathroom.

With the water running, Harry undresses and reflects upon his situation, stepping into the flow. Not much has changed. Rae's still gone, and he's still broke with nowhere to call home. He pushes all of that aside and reflects on his old poetry. If he's going to do a 'zine, then poetry was his thing before business came into the picture. It could work.

Then, it dawns on him: no one's said a word about Mercanary. That's a little odd, isn't it?

Mercanary appreciates the many uses of masks.

He returns to the kitchen wrapped in a small towel, and Mercanary is floating above the table, reading the comic strips in *The Herald*.

"Coo?"

"Almost. C'mon down to the shed." Harry grabs the key from the rack. "I'll get something to put on."

They go down the stairs that exit onto the back lot. It's empty, but a car pulls in. Someone who must work in the plaza. They cross in front of the car, and the driver glares.

Harry doesn't notice. He unlocks the padlock, flips the latch, and swings open the double doors. Inside, the shed is packed with boxes and garbage bags, a pair of mattresses without a bed frame, and a highboy. There's almost no room left to get to the stand-up freezer, never mind the blue tarp.

"I'll just be a minute or two. Don't touch anything."

Harry rummages through his things, tossing

aside boxes and tearing open the garbage bags just to check the contents inside, and Mercanary opens the freezer.

"COO!" Mercanary yelps standing between the opened doors. "COO! COO! COO! COO! COO!"

Frozen chicken carcasses fill it. Mercanary's eyes are wide with horror. His tongue whips about frantically with each coo.

"Dude! What's wrong?" Harry gets his answer when he sees the beast examining his departed kin, holding breasts in his wings. "Shit. I said don't touch anything, right?"

"COO! COO! COO!"

"Yeah, yeah. I understand, but this is a part of life, right?"

"COO! COO! COO! COO! COO! COO!"

"Okay! Okay! I know what you mean," Harry tries to console the trembling creature, placing his left arm around the seabird's feathery shoulders, his right hand still clutching the towel around his waist. "There's nothing I can say that will bring them back. This is just how things are. People eat birds sometimes. Holy shit, Newfies eat fish, too, and –"

"COOOOOOOOO!" Mercanary wails, Harry throws up his hands to cover his ears, and his towel slips off to the floor. The driver from a moment earlier walks past to see a naked Harry yelling into the freezer.

Mercanary appreciates the tranquil ritual of poetry at this time of the year.

The man shakes his head, walking around to the front of the plaza.

"No, no, no. Don't get like that. These things are sort of a way of life here, but not everyone eats chicken and fish."

"Coo?"

"Well, a few people don't eat meat, right? Like, they totally exist here, too."

"Chirp?"

"Yeah!"

"Chirp? Chirp?"

"That's right, man. Look, when in Rome, you act like the Romans. You know what I mean?"

"Coo."

"No? Well, what if I agree to do a 'zine? Will that keep you quiet?"

"CHIRP!" Mercanary beams at Harry again, putting the carcasses back, and closing the freezer doors.

"Shit. That was easier than I expected."

"Chirp, chirp! Chirp?"

"I used to write poetry when I was a kid. I was thinking I'd write a little poetry 'zine. What do you thi–"

"CHIRP! CHIRP! CHIRP!"

"Great! I didn't think you'd get so excited about amateur poetry."

"Chirp!"

"Yeah, well, a lot of people don't like any poetry."

"CHIRP!"

"Just like a lot of people eat meat, hunh? You got me there. I guess a few are just going to have to be enough to be satisfied with."

"Chirp, chirp, chirp."

"Yeah. I'll get it done. We'll figure it out. Look, all I have is $4, and it's like another three weeks until this 'zine fair thing. Let me get my things and say goodbye, and then I think we'll just have to disappear to get this done. I'm already off everyone's radar since Rae left. Fuck it. We'll put in a long haul camping out around Signal Hill. I need time and space like this. I know a few spots we can tuck in at night. It won't be too rough. I'll take my backpack, too."

After collecting his things and locking up the shed and apartment, Harry says so long to Marg. Bob hasn't returned yet. He gives her the same tale he's given each of his friends: he's grateful for the assistance; he has errands to run; he'll see people; he'll find somewhere to spend the night. The way he says it, it's not exactly a lie, but he's not telling the truth, either. Marg knows the difference, but she also knows you can't really argue with Harry when he's set on his course. She hugs him, and then waves from the restaurant's entrance as Harry and Mercanary mosey off toward downtown.

Mercanary appreciates a sweet treat for strange friends in such peculiar times.

The next three weeks are a blur of reflecting, bellyaching, writing, struggling, and surviving. It is much rougher than Harry estimated, but, like, we needn't detail every uncomfortable shit and the mess of leaves he left beside each pile.

Still, Mercanary keeps him company, and they manage, salvaging food scraps from dumpsters downtown and sleeping in little hideaways along the hiking trails near Signal Hill and Quidi Vidi. Moved by Mercanary's naive enthusiasm, Harry's spirits are higher than one would expect, and he scratches notes into the dirt with a stick when his spirits are at their highest. After erasing and re-writing, Harry drafts each of his works on his laptop. Sparing the charge in its battery as much as he can, he only checks his Farcebark and Immedia accounts long enough to like a few posts. This is so people know he's still alive.

By the middle of the second week, Harry starts fastening his belt a notch tighter. By the end of the third week, he's another notch tighter. He's not too bothered. He can afford to lose those inches and pounds.

Mercanary appreciates things just might be easier if he were Krazy.

He hasn't spent his $4 yet, not even for a coffee or a few smokes. He gets by with public tapwater and bumming draws from strangers on the street downtown. That $4 is locked-in for another purpose now.

The day before the 'zine fair, Harry and Mercanary visit Copy Matters for the moment of truth.

It's not crowded inside, but the air is thick with humidity; the sea of copiers generate that stickiness. There's a hipster dude behind the counter. His eyes widen as the two step up.

Harry hasn't shaved in weeks, his beard's motley, his hair's scraggly and beginning to dread, and he hasn't showered in all this time, so he may as well reek of harbour water again.

"Can I help you?"

"Yeah, so I only have this $4," Harry admits as he sets the three coins on the countertop, "and I need to print off copies of this 'zine. It's just a document. A single page. Double-sided."

"Okay. We have coin-op machines in the front there." He points across the room to the farthest corner near the front of the copy shop.

"Yeah, but I don't know how to print this off so it'll fold right. Like, can you do a test one for me?"

The clerk begins to moan but cuts himself off, attempting to maintain some degree of customer service. "Not for free. Black and white is 8 cents a page, and –"

"Black and white'll do."

"Give me your jump drive. And double-sided is 12 cents."

"Right. It's still on my laptop. Got a cable?"

"Ugh. Just email the file."

"Can I get on your Wi-Fi?"

Harry and the clerk sort out the document delivery while Mercanary entertains himself by swooping circles around the rows of copiers. Besides detecting Harry's stench after they entered, the other customers continue copying their own matters.

The first test is misaligned, as Harry had feared. The clerk adjusts the double-sided settings, but they print two more mismatched pages before getting the front and back to align when folded into an octavo. The clerk doesn't offer a discount for the errors, and Harry doesn't bother to ask.

For $4, Harry recieves a stack of 27 copies of his 'zine. He just has to fold, staple, and cut the lot of them.

"That stapler, those scissors – I can use those here, yeah?"

"Yeah, but if you're sticking around, you'll have to do it away from the other customers. You know you stink, right?"

Harry blinks at the clerk and takes the tools to the side of the shop, where he sits on the floor, folding, stapling, and cutting his 'zines. Mercanary flops to the floor beside him, swishing his tail along the side of the wall.

"Chirp, chirp!"

"I know! It's a real thing now, this 'zine," Harry agrees, "but it's gonna take a few hours to finish this batch."

"Coo. Chirp."

Harry's busy with his work, and he doesn't notice the time passing or other customers coming and going. Mercanary remains at his side, fiddling with everything within reach. No one bothers them.

Then, he notices a woman's voice complaining about the stink.

"Christ, Tyler! You shit yourself or wha?"

"SHH!" Tyler responds sharply, adding, "The

stink's still here."

"Shit. Those brunch menus ready?"

"Totally. Let me get that for you!"

Tyler is eager to please, and Harry guesses he has a thing for this lady that goes beyond brunch menus. He peeps over the copiers, curious.

She's leaning into the counter and back-on to Harry. He takes his time to admire the view of her slim and styled figure. Clad in black tights and a black vest with a white blouse peeking though, he thinks she looks more like a hostess than a server. She's a redhead, too, with her hair tied back in a ponytail that stretches down between her shoulder blades. She leans over further, impatiently waiting Tyler's return, and she lifts one leg, letting her shoe dangle while bobbing her foot slightly.

"Fuck," Harry whispers to Mercanary, who swings around to see what's what.

"Chir-r-r-r-R-R-R-R-R-R-R-RP!"

"Keep it down, dude!"

Harry pushes Mercanary down and slinks lower himself. Mercanary bounces back up for another look. She turns, and Harry ducks. Mercanary gawks still, unconcerned.

Did she see him?

Mercanary appreciates the intent in such stealth missions as well as the irony in a gag.

She doesn't acknowledge either of them, so Harry remains silent and hidden – basically holding his breath – until she's left, and then he finishes making 'zines.

It's almost dark when they leave Copy Matters behind. He decides to stick around the streets of downtown until morning to be as bright-eyed and bushy-tailed as he can manage in order to get through the day at the House of Broken Books.

Harry knows to make the most of his urban surroundings. There are places one can accomplish what one needs if one knows where to look. He brings Mercanary to the Omega Hotel, located at the west end of downtown. They scout out the lobby from the sidewalk across the road on Barter's Hill, waiting for a group of guests with whom he might fit in.

It's dark when two taxi-vans pull up to the hotel's entrance. The passengers get out, and Harry's relieved that alt-rock's not dead in this town, because this is his best shot. A band of grungy punks unload some gear and luggage from the vans, and Harry leads Mercanary closer.

No one else has seen this fantastic creature yet, Harry thinks, so this just might work.

The two trail the band into the lobby of the Omega – far enough behind them so they won't notice, but close enough behind them so the bellhops won't suspect he's not a guest. Only one goes to check-in, and the others head straight for the elevators. Harry sidles away from them. With Mercanary floating along behind him, he goes straight for the pool.

Sure enough, there's no fuss about Mercanary fluttering about – not from the staff and not from the other guests.

What gives?

The duo move down a hallway, following the signs. Energy-saving lights flicker on as they near the pool's showers. A viewing window shows the pool's not being used, as far as Harry can see, which is useful.

"Okay. Look, I'm going to grab a shower, a long shower, and I need you to stick around and not freak anyone out."

"COO!"

Mercanary looks hurt.

"It's not like that. You're amazing, but people fear what's different, what they don't know. Ya know?"

"Coo."

"Yeah, but you'll learn."

This is not as reassuring as it sounds.

Harry continues, "You can go for a swim in the pool if you like, no one's in –"

Before he can finish, Mercanary bolts.

The door to the pool area swings open, as if pushed by a great force, and Mercanary swoops inside, rising higher than the water slide and swan-diving into the shallow end.

Harry shakes his head and enters the men's changing room. He finds a spot near the back where he lays down his satchel and backpack, then he quenches his thirst by lapping up water from the sink. He dries his hands with brown paper towels, and then he douses them with liquid hand soap. It'll have to do. He undresses and takes the soapy paper towels into the shower with him and tries to scrub off three weeks of filth.

This time, he only thinks about his new friend. Although he's puzzled, these aren't troubling thoughts. He's glad this beast-thing has come into his life. What would he have done without him, honestly?

It's more like an hour later when Harry enters the pool area to retrieve his friend. A woman lounges by the pool, fully clothed, scrolling something on her phone as two young children swim and play on the water slide.

Mercanary is not swimming.

Harry's alarmed.

He scans the water again and then the poolside, but there's no Mercanary to be seen.

"Oh, shit!" Harry exclaims, drawing looks from the adult and the children. "Sorry. I thought I'd left something in here earlier. I don't see it here now, though."

The others don't care. The kids go back to playing and the woman returns to scrolling.

Harry pivots on his heel to leave, and then a feather falls right under his nose. He looks up to see Mercanary hanging by his mer-tail from the girders high above. His wings are outstretched as if this is some masterful yoga pose.

He shoots him that look that signals *c'mon*, hoping Mercanary will understand to meet him outside, and that's when fin-n-feather fades from sight altogether.

What the fuck?

Harry throws up his hands, lets out a sigh, and returns to the hallway.

Mercanary doesn't appear.

Harry waits.

Still no Mercanary.

Harry leaves the hotel, but waits outside where they were scouting the lobby earlier. He waits there for more than an hour.

Still no Mercanary.

Finally, he leaves. He needs some rest for

tomorrow. He should try to be alert enough to hawk a few of these 'zines, so he decides to tuck into the entrance of a bank to sleep for the night. The bankers lock that foyer, sure, but the first door is open as long as you have a bank card. Placing his satchel and bag in the corner of the porch, Harry uses them as a pillow, and he sleeps.

Harry's nightmares return.

A swirling grey sky canopies his whole world as he walks a winding road full of potholes. There's no end, and it feels as if he has been walking for years without reaching his destination. There is no destination in sight. There's not much of anything welcoming within view. The landscape is a shifting void of barrens and rocks.

Harry feels a figure stalking him, but whenever he dares to look, the presence can't be found.

It mocks him with shrill laughter from the abyss as the road crumbles and Harry plummets.

He doesn't wake immediately, and his muscles are tense when he gets up in the morning.

The door opens. Harry looks up a bit too eagerly, and the man entering the bank gives a little jump. The stranger uses the ATM without speaking, preferring to ignore this homeless dude on the floor, of course.

Harry gets up, gathers his things, and leaves to set up at the 'zine fair before the man is finished banking.

The morning goes well enough, but Harry misses Mercanary. He still has so many questions, but he tries to be cheerful enough to sell some of his 'zines.

The proprietor of the bookshop, Matthieu Manse, is a godsend to the writers in the local scene. That means all of them, too. He opens up his space for these sorts of events each week, hosting launches and readings more than any other venue in the city. He's creating a community, and it's not like anyone else has the initiative or the heart to make it happen. All of this is on top of purchasing books from local authors rather than carrying them on consignment. That's a real boon for the amateurs. That kind of generosity really makes a difference.

Mr. Manse is the only one running the show today. If the poster girl works here, she's not in. Or she's just not in yet, Harry supposes.

Harry's sold nearly half of his stock – by the look of it – by noon. Most customers have been nice but shy. That's when some dude decides to chit-chat.

"This your 'zine?"

Of course it is. Harry's set up in an isolated corner of the shop, there by himself.

"Yeah! It's a 'zine of poetry and adventure that I

made. It took me weeks, actually. Maybe you'll dig it, dude."

"Ye-e-e-e-e-e-e-e-e-e-e-e-e-e-e-eah, nah."

Harry's caught off-guard somewhat. Dude looks like a douche.

"See, 'zines are cool. I was going to make a 'zine, but then I thought, 'Nah. Making a 'zine because there's some event, some prompt, some pop-up? That's not punk, so why bother?'"

"Right," Harry replies. "So, you didn't do one then?"

"Nah."

"Alright then. And you're not gonna buy one of mine?"

"Nah. Later."

The douche walks away, and Harry's more deflated than he would've expected, given such childish trolling.

The fair ends before supper, but it's not like Harry's eaten anything yet today. He devoted himself to this, and before packing up his things he takes a tally: 15 sold; 12 unsold; and, $30 earned.

It's a start, Harry thinks.

He smiles and nods at Mr. Manse across the room. A charitable smile is returned by the store's owner, and Harry leaves in search of a meal.

He decides to try his luck again back at the Omega. They have a dining room with a buffet for guests, and he just passed for a guest there last night.

For a bluff to succeed, one must look the part and act with confidence. Harry stashes his bags between a dumpster and the hotel's exterior, and then he musters up about all the gumption he has left to stroll in through the lobby.

No one stops him. He doesn't notice if anyone notices him or not, and he finds the dining room's buffet. It's all salads and sides.

He's famished. He collects a variety, takes a seat alone at a table, and tries not to eat it too quickly.

Chewing leaves, he scopes out the dining room. A couple in rich attire dine at one table, a well-rounded businessman dines alone at another, and a slim redhead returns to the hostess' podium. Mercanary's not arou – wait! That's the woman from Copy Matters!

Harry sits up straighter. He's growing anxious. Did she see him? Would she suspect he's not a guest? He can only maintain his scheme now; he's already in the middle of it.

She's busy with her own work, however, so Harry finishes his helpings and risks picking up more spinach salad from the buffet, like a regular guest.

The hostess looks up at his moving about, returns to her notes, but then she looks directly at him and asks, "Harry?"

Oh, fuck, Harry thinks.

He's lucky he's frozen in place because it helps him resist meeting her gaze.

"Is that you, Harry?"

Harry hasn't placed her voice, but he's not about to stick around to find out who recognizes him in the middle of stealing salad.

The plate drops. It shatters. Spinach scatters.

"Shit."

Harry runs, and the hostess shouts, "Hey! Stop! Someone stop that guy!"

Harry hasn't much to be at, but he has no time for this. It's a good thing he's been walking and hiking everywhere, because now he needs to run. Again.

Only one wanna-be-hero guest makes a grab for him, but Harry swerves and shoves a luggage cart into the guest's path. The Good Samaritan trips, kicking the cart into bystanders.

A bellhop blocks the entrance, but he's even scrawnier than Harry. That poor kid gets a solid push to the ground as Harry runs through him.

"Sorry," Harry calls out over his shoulder.

A few bold men stand at the entrance, as if it marks the threshold of their obligations, and they watch Harry run around the corner without pursuing him. He's not worth the effort to any of them. None of the would-be heroes help the bellhop to his feet.

Harry slows to a jog, nearing the dumpster where he left his bags.

They're gone.

Harry looks around in a panic. No one's back here with him besides a stray cat. He climbs into the dumpster, tossing garbage left and right, but it's only filled with trash and none of it's his. There's not even a Mercanary to be found inside.

A dark cloud obscures the moon's light. He slumps down against the bin, and he weeps without restraint.

This cry has been long overdue. The weight of it all bears down on him. He thought he had nothing before. There's even less now.

Harry cries for maybe 20 minutes, but another two hours pass before he crawls out of that dumpster.

The clothes on his back, the worn-out Chucks on his feet, an uncharged phone in his pocket, and the day's earnings are all he has remaining.

It's after midnight when he wanders along the downtown streets to a pay phone.

He's not thinking clearly, but his hands pick up the receiver and dial a number – collect.

An older woman answers, "Hello? Who's this? It's late, you know."

He greets her, "Mom? It's Harry."

The Birthing of the Beast-Thing

It was 2019 in this fowl year of our lord when the House of Broken Books, a local institution of the literati, put forth this call to adventurers: "LET THERE BE 'ZINES!"

And so, souls both foolish and brave set forth in search of 'zines, to relish in their bloody contents.

One such searcher was Donkey Reynolds, who was nearly blind and mostly dumb.

Blundering along the foggy coastal cliffs, he heard a fierce cooing and an erratic splashing down by the breakwater. The harbour's symphony stopped for only a moment, then machine-gun fire filled the air!

Unbeknownst to him, he had witnessed the birth of Mercanary, the mythical singer of songs, swimmer of seas, freelance fighter of freedoms, and herald of perplexing joys to come!

Mercanary was born fully matured and armed to the beak. His mission was clear: ensure Reynolds survives this 'zine challenge.

Together, Mercanary and Reynolds crossed land and sea on many a misadventure, with Reynolds occassionally asking inane and pointless questions of the seabird.

"What are ya at?"

"Where are you from?"

"Who owns you, sure?"

"Can you even breathe underwater without gills?"

"How can you pull a trigger with those massive wings?"

"Have you heard that Great Big C song about the mermaid?"

"What the fuck?"

"Are we there yet?"

And to every question Reynolds asked the beast-thing, Mercanary replied, "CHIRP, CHIRP! COO, COO!"

By the end of the day, they had reached home, a crooked piece of rock in the middle of the sea that the locals called Atlantis.

From the tip of Atlantis, Mercanary sees all, yet he dreads only one thing, his archnemesis, Troll-Cat, a vile and shameless creature that never bothered to make a 'zine but talks shit anyway.

Troll-Cat, Mercanary's archnemesis.

Grounded

The bus ride from St. John's to Harbour Grace takes nearly three hours with all the stops along the way. It costs $12.

Harry's taken a seat at the back of the bus. He was the first to board, and the other passengers keep their distance once they figure out he smells like a dumpster.

It's Sunday evening, and Harry hasn't slept since Friday night at the ATM. He's exhausted, but his mind's racing.

What can he tell them?

They're not going to be pleased. They always liked Raelyn. They blame him that she's gone. Maybe they're right.

Then, what happened to Mercanary?

Can anyone else see him?

What is Mercanary, anyway?

And then, what will he do in his hometown?

Are any of his old friends even still around out there?

How will he manage to get along with his parents?

He's lucky they'll let him come back, he thinks, and so on.

The bus drives past the *S.S. Kyle,* forever grounded in the harbour, and Harry discovers the fact that he's back in his hometown.

The bus stops at the liquor store on Main Street in Harbour Grace. This is where Harry gets off. His parents live further up the road behind the liquor store. The road's name never caught on with anyone in town; it's just called the Pipe Track, since the town's water main runs along underneath straight to its source.

Harry takes his time walking up the Pipe Track. The sky is a heavy overcast, a recent shower leaves the ground soaked, and it's just after supper. No one is out in the neighbourhood. It's just as well.

He walks past an abandoned church and an old, unused shoppe and all the other homes until he reaches his parent's house, a modest bungalow with red and white siding. Was it meant to be patriotic? In all his life, Harry had never asked. A hand-carved wooden sign beside the front step reads "The Buellers'."

He climbs the wet lawn's embankment to his parent's house as well as the steps to the front door.

He knocks.

His father swings open the door. "You're a stranger," he says to Harry.

"I know."

His father – Elvis, the coach, the boss, the king of the castle – turns without holding the door.

Harry feels like a vampire that requires a clear invitation to come in, but it's not exactly there. The door is open, so he enters.

His mother, Elvira, is in the kitchen. They've already eaten, and she's already cleaned up. She calls out from the other room, "Your sisters' room is all set. I cleared it all out this afternoon. You can put your things in there, and then come out for your supper before it's froze."

"He hasn't got any things, Elvy."

"Dad. I was robbed."

"Right," says Elvis, followed by a huff.

Harry knows it is difficult returning home. They see this as a failure. They must, and it's not his first failure. They have always been keen to remind him of that. The joblessness, Raelyn leaving, the couch surfing, the return home to mooch – it's merely the latest in a long series of failures, Harry thinks.

He hasn't heard the end of it yet, either. He's well aware of the price of staying at home. This is Elvis' house, where Elvis rules. Harry must remain as submissive as he can manage just to maintain some sense of peace. He's familiar with playing this role.

It's not like he's entirely ungrateful. These people raised him. They clothed him, fed him, and sheltered him. Certainly, they made more than one sacrifice over the years to give Harry some comforts – toys, cassette tapes, records, books, games, and more. Plus, they're taking him in again now. Harry loves them, deeply and truly.

But families are complicated, and all of the feelings are on the table. On this night, that table's in the kitchen.

While eating, Harry tells his parents a story. It's a true story, but he leaves out a lot of the details. He can't bear to be entirely truthful with them. It hurts too much to let his mother down. He tells them enough, and he doesn't cry in front of his father.

He hears it all, though, and it's not very pretty.

It takes most of that evening to satisfy his

parents' interrogation, but Harry lives through it. He thinks it went well, actually, but that's speaking relatively.

Once they've had enough, Harry cleans off his plate, glass, and cutlery in the sink. His mother supervises him, providing instructions, as if it was his first time washing dishes. Harry doesn't complain. He holds his tongue, and then excuses himself to get some sleep in one of his sisters' beds.

Eve and Emma, Harry's sisters, are away. They teach English overseas. They've been away seven years or so and only ever return to visit for one month each year. Some years they vacation elsewhere. They had always been super nice to Harry when he was little. He's really missed them these past years, but they're living the dream, pursuing a proper hero's journey with their lives, and they've gotten about as far from Harbour Grace as one can get without exiting the atmosphere. He can't begrudge them that. Harry's envious, but he just wants to sleep now, and he's thankful he can choose from their two beds.

He has another bad dream.

He's a youngster on the school bus, heading home after class. He's so little, and all the other children are bigger than he is. The others are monsters with vicious horns, oozing pustules, and gnarled teeth, but Harry's a human child, timid and frail. When he turns to look back, one scowling monster at the rear launches a pencil at Harry. It stabs into his left eye, and, as the monsters laugh, he screeches.

He actually screeches aloud, but he doesn't wake from such dreamt pain.

Elvis and Elvira wake, but they do not check on their son in the next room, presuming it will pass – like it always has.

The next day, Elvis gives Harry a ride to the mall in Carbonear where there's a walk-in barbershop.

"I'll be down da shore for four or five hours. If you wants a lift back home, text me before I'm back on da road."

"Gotcha. Thank you very much."

"Eh, b'y."

Elvis drives away as Harry looks around the parking lot. It's foggy, and the air feels dense. Some years have passed since he's been here, and – even with the new buildings, businesses, and roads – it's all too familiar still. He takes a deep breath and walks inside.

The Pirate's Cut pre-dates the birth of Harrison Stockton Bueller, and so does the decor. The front and back walls feature pirate scene murals that must've been there since the '70s or earlier.

There's a ship sailing through stormy waters, a bo'sun whipping lackeys, a cave where pirates unload booty, and one with a captain admirably guiding the rudder's wheel, his broad grin exposing golden teeth. None of the murals indicate the artist, and the adjoining walls are lined with mirrors and chairs, reminding clients this is actually a functioning salon.

Harry meets the young woman at the front desk. She recognizes him through his grizzly scruff and shaggy mop. Darlene's the younger sister of Nadine, and Nadine was in Harry's classes all through high school. Their mother, Emily Ayrehart, has owned this place most of Harry's life. They kept the branding as part of the turnkey takeover. Maybe it works for them.

This encounter becomes Harry's typical experience for the few hours he's puttering about the mall. It's only natural. People are curious. Harry's asked over and over:

"Why, it's been ages, hasn't it?"

"How've you been doing?"

"When did you get back home?"

"Where've you been?"

"What have you been doing with yourself?"

"Who are you shackin' up with these days?"

Harry knows he can't afford to rock the boat, so

he plays along coyly with his banter, answering questions with just enough of the truth to whet the locals' appetites.

"Indeed, it has."

"Best kind. I get by."

"Just last night."

"Town. Finished my business degree."

"Nah much, honestly. Tryin' to keep busy."

But Harry stumbles each time with that last sort of question. It's like it strikes him. His response varies throughout the day. He's looking for a good answer to this himself. Sure, each time someone asks him, he thinks of Rae, but that's not all of it. The people asking are asking so they might discern his relationship status, which just reads as "It's complicated" on his Farcebark profile. His stammer is a giveaway for anyone in town who knew him, and those people totally see Harry's heartbroken. It's all written plainly enough in the social math: Raelyn grew up in Carbonear, Harry's back here, and she's certainly not. Like, those who care to give it thought piece it together by the end of the day, but some catch on in his presence. This makes him uncomfortable, like he's being judged as some kind of impotent failure of a man.

Darlene caught on instantly, too. She's sharp, she's observant, and she's compassionate. Call it a knack or a hunch or her intuition, but she knows the score. Harry senses she does, but she doesn't press him on it. She gives him a proper trim and a shave for just $15. He thanks her warmly but, in the moment, thinks it's just the bay pricing, and he takes his last $3 to the mall's bar, The Shade, instead of tipping her.

The Shade is a tiny dive, to be clear, but it's a safe haven – a sort of shelter for the brokenhearted. It's basically just the bar, some stools, a pool table, the VLTs, and dimmed lighting. There's a door to the lot, but Harry comes in through the mall's entrance.

"S'up, Ian?"

"Nuttin'," replies the bartender before looking around from the sink behind the bar. He turns, "Geezus! Dat you, 'Arry?"

"Eh, b'y. Seems so."

Ian McReady was no joke back in high school. He was a hockey star, legendary even, if local folklore is to be believed. Ian's from Upper Island Cove, but he went to elementary school in Harbour Grace instead of Bay Roberts. Harry's relieved to see him. They got along well enough. Harry was just a punk then, but Ian never looked down on any of the weirdos or outsiders in those days. Harry respects that still.

Ian and Harry go through the typical banter, but Harry reveals more of the story when they get to the drama.

Raelyn's gone now. She'll have nothing more to do with him. Harry doesn't blame her. He's a bum, and she's got drive. He hasn't worked in months now, and the dole's run out already. He was living in her tiny one-room, but that's no longer an option. He's been couch-surfing for weeks, but that's just like treading water. He'd rather not think about any of it, and so he's come back, staying with his folks to look for some work. He has to find something to get him back on his feet.

Ian can relate. The first August after finishing high school, he was out jigging with his uncle on the far side of Harbour Grace Island, and that's when he injured his foot, which cost him a lifetime of preparation for a career playing hockey.

"... and I went over when dat wave rocked da boat –" He always gets flustered telling this story, and his accent grows thicker with the frustration.

"Holy shit!"

"– and Huncle Joe was the honly one d'ere, and 'e can't even swim, so 'e 'ooks me with this gaff 'e 'ad, and the way 'e 'ad dat 'ooked into me leg ... b'y, lemme tell you –"

"You are."

"– dat was d'end of it right d'ere. Dat twistin' an' yankin' me back into 'is rickety ole dory. End of it."

"Shit. I'd say. I'm sorry to hear, b'y." That's no lie. Harry would've liked to see Ian play professionally. This is it, though.

As the conversation slows, Harry twiddles two coins along the back of his fingers, a toonie and a loonie.

A decision is made, and Harry slinks over to a stool at one of the blinking VLTs.

"That one's lucky," says Ian from behind the bar.

"I bet ya say that to all the ladies." Harry chuckles, and Ian laughs too but doesn't get it. He has sense enough to laugh, all the same. He's a bartender, after all.

Harry sinks the toonie into the slot.

Seven spins later, he's down to his last dollar.

"Fuck."

"I know, man."

"Ian?"

"Wha?"

"Man, can I buy a couple singles off ya for a buck?"

"Price has gone up," Ian replies, handing him three smokes and taking the dollar.

"Dude, you don't have to tell me. Thanks. This

is a big help today."

Harry pulls up a stool at the bar, places a cigarette in his lips, raises his lighter, and Ian catches his hand.

"Outside."

"Right. Shit. I forgot, b'y. All this talk of the 'good ole days,' ya know?"

"Yeah. Outside, Harry."

"I'm on it." Harry moves toward the lot's entrance with the speed of someone jonesin', and he adds, "Thanks again! I'm sure I'll see ya around, buddy! Take 'er easy now!"

"If she's easy, maybe twice."

"Oh, ho, ho, ho!" Harry laughs, shaking his head as he steps onto the lot.

He lights and inhales. Exhaling, the smoke blends into the dense fog. He's walked home to Harbour Grace from Carbonear countless times before, but he hasn't the energy for it today. Climbing through that valley between the towns is worse than climbing up Barter's Hill, so he sends a text to his father for a lift home. He has hours left to spend being a mallrat.

One can't wander through the mall in Carbonear without running into people you know from all around this end of the bay. It's the only mall within an hour's drive, making Carbonear a mini-St. John's in its own little way. Never mind that there's a mall in Bay Roberts. Anyway, with each person that stops for a chat, Harry goes through the same speech, offering some but not all of his story. Ultimately, he's happy enough to put the word out that he's looking for work.

That evening, Harry is quick to inform his parents that he's going to need a job. They agree, but their comments are still critical. He accepts it. He deserves it, he thinks.

He updates his old resume that remains on the family's desktop PC and prints off a batch. Elvis said he could use the printer, but he'll have to replace the ink cartridges when he gets paid. Good enough, Harry thinks.

"Chirp, chirp! Coo, coo!"

– Quoth the Mercanary

There's too much on Harry's mind that he's not thinking about, and he can't sleep. It's late. His parents are sound. He shifts, rolls, turns, fidgets, jitters, and then gets out of bed, hauling a blanket and pillow behind him. He heads down the basement stairs without switching on any lights along the way. He moves as silently as a mouse might, feeling his way around the corner at the bottom. There, he tucks himself into the crawlspace, the only room in the house without a window. Curling up because he can't lie straight in this space, he eventually falls asleep on the cool

81

cement floor.

Another nightmare visits him that night.

He's his present age. Fuck, he's wearing today's clothes and sporting a fresh haircut, too, but he's in St. John's, wandering and wondering along all the broken streets and down every dark path. Grey day blends with greyer night and turns to grey day again without any break in Harry's stride or his consciousness. This is one of those nightmares where time is condensed but your thoughts move at a synchronous pace, and so it feels like an eternity is passing. He loses his job. She's gone. He's drunk. He trips. He staggers. He pukes. He wanders. He wonders. All of this he does through a dank fog smothering each night and with a loose mist clutching at the street each day. Then he walks through Harbourside Park, past the Terry Fox memorial, and into the sea. Storm clouds gather, and Harry looks to the beach. His gaze meets the grotesque visage of a troll-cat, sitting on the rocks, scowling at him. Troll-Cat growls and grows. It's becoming all that surrounds him. Its being permeates everything, reaching out from its sickly form, reaching out for Harry. He looks to the sky, expecting this fearsome creature's presence to consume the very gloaming.

That's when the storm clouds part. In the distant heights, Harry notices a tiny speck. It grows larger. It's moving quickly. As it nears, Harry recognizes Mercanary, dual machine guns under each outstretched wing, tail guiding his flight like a ship's rudder.

Mercanary plummets fearlessly from the heavens, sights set dead on Troll-Cat. He accelerates. The sonic boom is like no thunder Harry's ever heard, but Mercanary flies like a flash. The collision with Troll-Cat is explosive, waking Harry.

He bolts upright with a gasp, as if the air had been knocked out of him.

Beside Harry sits Mercanary, beaming smile just as generous as before, like nothing was missed. For the first time in years, Harry recalls a dream.

Mercanary appreciates we are all Bojack Horseman... or Todd-as-Bojack-praising-a-poor-simulacrum-of-Todd.

"Why, it's been ages, hasn't it?" Harry asks immediately.

"Coo. Chirp, chirp."

"How've you been doing?"

"Chirp!"

"When did you get back?"

"Coo."

"Where've you been?"

"Chirp. Coo. Chirp, chirp, chirp."

"What have you been doing with yourself there?"

"Coo. Coo, coo, Chirp!"

Mercanary appreciates one should not gaze into an abyss for too long.

"Wow! That's some story. Fuck." Harry's impressed, and he's thoroughly pleased that Mercanary's returned. "Wait. Listen. This is my parents' place. They can't see you. Got it?"

"Coo?"

"No, they won't want to give you the tour."

"Coo, coo?"

"Because they'd have a fit! You've gotta promise me you aren't here to cause a fuss. I need them. They're family. Please."

"CHIRP!"

"Yeah? Just like that, eh?" Harry's reluctant to accept Mercanary's claim of having the highest stealth scores at commando bootcamp, but he accepts this on faith. "Alright then. You're welcome to stay as long as no one notices you. Agreed?"

"CHIRP!"

With that, things begin looking up for Harry, and most of the year that follows is either good at its best or tolerable at its worst.

That very day Harry sets off in search of employment with Mercanary by his side. His parents are on his case each day about the job hunt, but that doesn't bother him with Mercanary keeping him company.

He lands a job the following week, which he starts two weeks after the interview. It's a year-long contract with an anti-bullying initiative. It's one of those make-work programs for youth at-risk. Harry's jobless period and homeless stint qualifies him as at-risk, but he's certain his degree gets him this one. In that sense, he's privileged. That's a given. Once his group finishes training, they are left to direct the program entirely on their own, and the consensus is that they'll develop a puppet show to take on a school tour. That's how they would disseminate the anti-bullying knowledge they gained to the youth all throughout the region. It was a wholesome message in disguise, a trick on its surface and a white lie at its heart. Harry wasn't just a puppeteer, however; he and the others had full ownership of this from start to finish. They wrote the script, they made the set, they designed the characters, and they stitched their own puppets from scratch, upcycling old junk in the process. And, through their puppets, each of these puppeteers were educators.

Harry would never admit just how influential this time would be on the reformation of his character, so don't ever ask him, but this gig is what leads him to writing a children's story, *The True Story of the Three Billy Goats Gruff: The Troll's Side of the Story*, and he even pitches it to publishers in town. More on this later.

Mercanary appreciates the culture, not the corporations.

Anyway, his spirits are much higher after accepting the job offer, and he's finding ways to spend his time without spending any money. He's reading again. Like, I mean he's reading a lot. Just about everything in the house with words in it or on it, he's reading it. He reads his mother's books, his father's books, his sisters' books, and even his own old books that he's read before. All the while, he's reading to Mercanary, teaching the seabird about pop culture and humanity. This brings him to a stack of old fantasy-styled, choose-your-own-way adventure books. Harry's always adored these branching narratives, and – perhaps because of Mercanary's sheer glee at everything – the experience helps kindle a fire in him that was doused long ago.

He's reconnected with some more of his old friends, the geekier ones, and he begins hosting a tabletop roleplaying game with the brothers Iggy and Jack Everhard, and Darlene, who's excited to accept the spot Nadine had rejected. She had never played anything like this before, so it's entirely new to her, and what's new is thrilling.

Mercanary appreciates attraction but knows
there are no laws.

Five weeks after moving in with his folks,
Harry replaces the printer's ink. This does little to
improve their view of him, but Harry's still
working on it. He speaks with his sisters
occasionally – phone calls on birthdays and
holidays and the like. He tries his best to be jovial,
and it's not too much of a stretch for Harry at this
point. Things are improving.

Seven weeks pass, and Harry buys an old
beater, a 323, with his second paycheque before he
begins putting some savings aside. The car has
nearly 300,000 kms on the odometer when he gets
it from a neighbour on the cheap, a private sale.
It's nothing impressive, but it gets him around on
his own, relieving some of the burden he feels he's
placed on his parents and freeing himself from
another degree of relying on Elvis.

Then again, maybe the wheels are impressive
on some level, because eight weeks after moving
home, Harry and Darlene begin dating. Their first
date was taking in a retro film at the cinema in
Carbonear – *Universal Soldier*. It was her first
time seeing it. She found it shocking. He found her
reaction electrifying.

That's the night of their first kiss. It's entirely
innocent with an implied patience. It's
straightforward: he gives her a ride to the

Ayreharts', an awkward moment passes as they're parked, she gets out of the car with a "Good night" and a smile, she closes her door, Harry bursts from the driver's-side door, scoots around the hatchback, snatches her hand, spins her, their eyes meet, they're embraced, and they kiss – long, wet, and smooth – and then they part for the night, each slightly aglow.

This relationship is good for them.

That is, for a time.

It's Guy Fawkes' Night now, the second since Harry's return, and the couple are attending the bonfire on the beach near the *Kyle*. Mercanary entertains himself by delighting the local children. He swoops through the fire, which causes flames and children to dance alike.

Darlene has been a little distant since their last game with Iggy and Jack.

"... and then my rabbit takes the lion aside, they bond, and – what's up? Are you even listening?"

"What? Oh, no," Darlene replies.

"You've been weird all week. Is something wrong? Like, you're acting a little distant, right?"

"It's nothing. I'm fine."

"Okay." Harry's about to let it slide, but he can't resist. He thinks he must've done something wrong, and he pokes her, asking, "Did I do something wrong?"

"Well, it would've been cool if you had my back at the game table." She pulls away from him to look him straight in the eye.

"I thought the game was going well! Pass and Kron took down that troll after. Your plan – Nihilisa's plan to use liquid fire – the plan worked, and you had heals covered. I dunno. What do you mean?"

"You made me roll for loot against Jack."

"Yeah. So?"

"For a healing wand. I'm the party's healer."

"Okay. But, Pass is a bard-type, and they're good as back-up heals, like if Nihilisa's knocked down or elsewhere or whatever."

"So, you think Nihilisa's gonna let them down, yeah? Figured."

"What? No! That's not what I meant."

"You're the one who told me to be the healer."

"You could've said no. You could've played another type –"

"I didn't know anything about what I could or couldn't do! You led me to playing that healer!"

"Yeah, because Kron is the tank and Pass is damage and back-up hea–"

"Heals. Right. I've got your heals." She sounds meaner than Harry'd ever heard her.

"I know you do."

"You don't know shit."

"What the fuck is that for?"

"If you don't know by now, then I'm done trying to explain."

"What does that mean?"

"It means I'm going home. Without you. Gonna get a ride." Darlene gets off Harry's blanket, and she walks away.

Harry's sitting there, a little dumbfounded.

Mercanary's still delighting children when he notices Darlene's left Harry, and then he glides onto the blanket in Darlene's place.

"What the fuck just happened?"

"Coo. Coo, coo, coo. Chirp?"

"No. I don't expect she's coming back."

"Coo?"

"Yeah."

"Coo, coo, coo."

"I think that's it, Mercanary. Shit. No lover wants to be treated fairly. Lovers need to feel special. Fuck. I'm a slow learner."

"Chirp, chirp, chirp!"

"Yeah. Learning eventually is better than never learning at all. I know, you're right, but it's not easy, b'y."

"Coo. Chirp!"

"Thanks. C'mon, we goes home."

Harry takes his time picking up. He's deliberately being slow to see that Darlene actually catches a ride. Fuck. She had best not try to hitch back home tonight, he thinks. He spies her with Nadine through the bonfire's flames. Nadine gives him a grimace as she puts her arm around her sister, and they leave together.

Harry sighs and scoops up the blanket. He and Mercanary mosey back to the 323.

Harry's sleeping soundly since Mercanary came back to him, and this night is no different.

Things can always get worse, though, and sometimes they do.

Monday morning is never the best time to process a break-up, not while at work, and especially not when work goes like this.

Harry's getting through the day, doing his best, but a young boy, aged 8 or 9, approaches him as he's dismantling the puppet's stage.

Mercanary appreciates this brand of content is not fit to suit everyone's tastes.

I'm not about to reveal that poor child's story. It's too, too much. Even for me. Use your imagination if you really want to fill in this blank, because I feel that child's story is his own, and it's absolutely none of our business.

Our business here – if we have any kind of business here – is with Harry, and he's crushed. Mercanary weeps from behind the teacher's desk, unnoticed. What can they do? They didn't train them for this, and the boy's caught him unprepared and ill-equipped to help.

Harry seeks out the boy's homeroom teacher, and defers him to her. She calls in a social worker, and Harry waits with the young boy. They chat about cartoons like *G.I. Joe, Robotech,* and *Tales from the Crypt*, steering clear of cartoons like *Teddy Ruxpin* or *Care Bears*.

The social worker arrives two hours later.

It's out of his hands. He'll never hear how that boy's story unfolds, and I'm keeping it from you, as well.

Mercanary appreciates one may be curious.

Harry puts in his two-weeks' notice less than an hour after passing the boy on to someone who might be able to do something. I've already told you. It was too much.

Harry calls the Everhards. He says the campaign is over and they might get weird looks from Darlene for a while. He apologizes on her behalf, presumptively, and suggests they give her some space. Iggy and Jack get it. This isn't the first campaign to end this way. More or less, they each tell him to keep his chin up. He doesn't tell them why he really quit his gig. Let them suppose he's heartbroken over Darlene, he thinks. Sure, he's still not over Rae.

Mercanary appreciates some lightning and thunder.

That night, the terrors haunt his sleep.

It's a repeat episode.

He's a child.

He's in the forest.

It's dark and damp and cold and threatening.

A perverse presence clutches him from behind. This time, Harry recognizes it. Troll-Cat leans over his shoulder, grasping Harry's waist. A grotesque tongue lolls about Harry's earlobe, licking and slimy.

Harry cringes, shivering and shrivelling.

That's when there's a piercing cry, as if from an eagle or an owl or some other fearsome flying descendent of velociraptors.

Harry dares to look up, and he's rewarded with a vision of Mercanary.

Mercanary's pitch shifts, both his cry and his trajectory. The shrieking sound becomes a bellow, like Moby-fuckin'-Dick's own whalesong battlecry, as Mercanary's dive levels with the leafy forest floor.

SWOOP, SWOOP!

Mercanary appreciates the wonder of a hit and the timing must be opportune.

Troll-Cat's snatched by Mercanary in a fly-by.

Tears roll down Harry's face.

It's not sadness he feels – more like poetic justice – and the remainder of this dream consists of Mercanary's mighty smackdown on Troll-Cat. The battle is fierce, back-and-forth. It is not easy, but Mercanary appears triumphant when Troll-Cat flees into a tiny hovel in the ground beneath a tree.

When Harry awakes in his sister's bed, Mercanary is sitting on the other.

"Thanks," Harry greets his friend warmly. Mercanary beams a beaky smile at his friend, and that's the end of that.

Mercanary appreciates that, though he may be small, he may yet make a potent impact.

Over breakfast, Harry tells his parents that he put in his notice. He doesn't tell them the real reason, either. They tell him how foolish he is to quit his job over a break-up. He accepts whatever they throw at him. There's no way he's sharing the truth with anyone.

Besides drinking socially and smoking regularly, Harry hasn't done any drugs since the mushrooms and the pink robots. Today, he scores a few grams of weed. He feels he needs it. It's medicine. He's trying to cope. Scoring's no trouble. Iggy's always smoking joints, and Harry gets hooked up before supper.

After supper with his parents, Harry goes to the basement. This is where he reads to Mercanary, and his folks almost never bother them. In the old study, Harry fishes his bong from its hiding place, which is simply a box in a stack of boxes. He fills it with some water from the sink in the laundry room, then returns to the study with Mercanary and lights up.

Guggle, guggle, guggle goes the bubbling water bong as Harry takes a long and dirty haul from this ancient relic of his teenage years.

He stymies a cough, and says to Mercanary, "Shit. I hope they can't hear this thing."

Of course, the walls are like paper, and everything is heard.

Just a minute after he first hits the bong, Harry's mother enters without knocking.

"What's that sound, Harry?" But she sees what it is, and follows up, yelling, "Harry! What are you doing? Is that dope?"

"It is."

"Harry, don't turn to drugs just because Darlene and you had a fight. You could win her back. Have you even tried?"

"Mom, I –" He would've said he needs it to cope with the break-up – a lie – and that weed's no big deal – the truth – but his mother continues.

"What will people say? They'll say we raised a delinquent. That's what they'll all say."

"Mom, I –" He would've said he doesn't think people would say that or even think it. And why has she made this about her parenting so suddenly like that? He's puzzled by her approach.

"And what's Elvis gonna say about this? He'll hit the roof, you know."

"Mom, I –" He would've said that Elvis might understand what he's going through. Again, his mother doesn't let him get it out.

"Harry! You're grounded!"

"What?"

"Yes, you're grounded. Go to your room."

"What the fuck, Mom?"

"You need to learn! How else can we teach you? Go to your room!"

"Mom. I'm moving out."

"What? But, why?"

"Listen. I'm going to go back to town. I can leave tonight and find somewhere to crash, or I can stay here until I put in my last couple of weeks. It's your call, but if you and Dad can't give me some fucking time and space to process this shit, then I'm out, and I can leave within the hour."

"Now, you give that up! I've got some of those Semi-Sweet Rosebuds. They're your favourite. Come upstairs and have a treat."

"What? Mom, I –"

"Harry," Elvira says with the greatest gentleness, "Don't go. We don't want you to go. Why would you think that?"

"Are you for real?"

"What do you mean, Harrison?"

"Mom, I need you and Dad to react to my crises with a little more compassion. Shit. And you can't ground an adult. What was that about?"

"You're my baby."

"No, Mom. Once upon a time, yes. I'm your son, but I've become a man."

Has he?

Harry can't bear to let Elvira see him cry, not after delivering a line like that, so he takes his bong out to the shed. Mercanary follows along behind him. He finishes this bowl and packs another for Mercanary, passing it.

Elvira doesn't tell Elvis about the weed. The evening isn't as rough as Harry had expected. His mother really came through in the end. His father suspects he's missing a piece of the puzzle, but he doesn't search for it. There's a certain wisdom in letting the right things slide, but you have to commit to the action based on a hunch. Harry inherited a great deal of wisdom from both of them, even if it wasn't always easy learning such lessons.

Mercanary appreciates the seas nearly as much as a good spoon.

The next day, Harry reaches out to his friends in St. John's.

He gives them the lowdown. He lost his girl, and he's without work again. It's the same old story, isn't it?

He catches up on their news. Marg tells him Bob's been seeing a man about a horse more frequently. He's away when Harry calls. Every three weeks or so, he goes on another one of these trips. She's been holding down the fort while he's away.

Elsewhere, Vince continues his lectures and research. Patti's living with him now, and they're having a grand time. She's fronting a punk band that plays shows downtown. Things still feel fresh for them, and they're thriving.

None of them have any leads on rooms or work. They aren't looking for these things, so it makes sense. Work can wait, Harry figures. He has $6,138 in his savings account, and that ought to see him through the first few months if he needs to rely on it.

Bob calls Harry three days later.

"Bro, I hear you're in need," Bob's voice sounds as one that delivers buoyant spirits.

"I am. Marg's told you, right? Ya know for a room or some work or wha?"

"That, I do, bro."

"Fuckin' right, Bob! You da man! Whatcha got?"

"The job's perfect for you. Courier sound dece' or wha?"

"Not bad. You're right. And the room?"

"You're gunna looooove this one."

"Fuck. Don't build suspense. Where is it?"

"The where hardly matters 't all. The who will pique your interest."

"Who, man? Who's got a room I can rent? Bob, yer killin' me here."

Untitled

Words.

Fuck words!

Fuckin' words.

Word?

On Exhibition

Exhibiting art is like casting a stone into a raging river. The stone is your contribution. Once it is cast, it's out of your hands as the river engulfs it. The river is the entire body of work in that artistic realm, and the current is how people view it. Odds are that the river's current will erode your stone, leaving it as a pebble or a grain of sand, a speck of little significance. Yet it is never insignificant, and some stones, when conditions are right, somehow calcify, growing to become more than the stone when it was thrown.

In Youth

The True Story of the Three Billy Goats Gruff:
The Troll's Side of the Story

ILLUSTRATION GUIDE FOR *THE TRUE STORY...*

SETTING: It's sort of like a valley; there are two hillsides with a brook trickling through between them. A stone bridge crosses over the brook, and the troll lives under the bridge. The grassiest side of the valley is the far side. The goats must cross the bridge to graze on the lushest grass.

THE TROLL: The original is described like this: "...under the bridge lived a great ugly Troll, with eyes as big as saucers, and a nose as long as a poker." Our troll should resemble this, too, but he should look a little friendlier. I figure he can look all kinds of ugly, but his saucer eyes should be more kind and sympathetic. And, he should come off as friendly when he smiles and helps the goats.

THE GOATS GRUFF: Our goats should each look gruff, kind of shaggy, to really emphasize their namesake. OH! And, they need to have those crazy goat eyes ████. I'm reminded of Crazy goat eyes are a must. Haha! When I think of ██████████ one who's actually ████ Dickens██████ y Tim or the youngest cousin ████████████████ little brother in real life... anyways, the youngest Gruff makes me think of those two, just in cartoony goat form. Maybe the youngest Gruff wears thick-rimmed glasses. The teenage Gruff rides a skateboard (maybe standing upright, or maybe on all fours, whichever ██ ██ s funniest). I picture a goat inspired b██████████ skate ████ riding ████ed d██ minion dock and wearing goofy ████ ██ or he's sort of like ██, the oldest Gruff should be a bit more psychotic looking. ██ psychotic Gruff. ████ ██ represents ignorance and leaping to violence for a solution. He's a beefhead and a douche. He's the villain of this piece.

DIMENSIONS

COVER – H 8.5" W 17" (the left half is the back, and the right half is the front cover of the book)

INTERIOR PAGES – H 8.5" W 8.5" (14 pages)

103

The True Story of the Three Billy Goats Gruff: The Troll's Side of the Story - COVER

One spring morning on my vacation, I was resting under the bridge.

Then I heard someone come near the bridge. Whoever it was he was tramping very hard.

I went on top of the bridge to see who it was. It was the youngest billy goat Gruff.

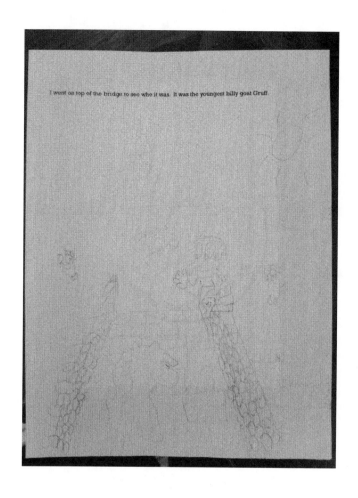

The Gruffs are very weird. He saw me and jumped over the side of the bridge with fright.

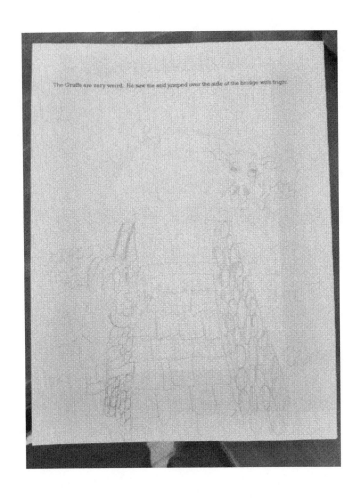

I had to help him out of the water. It was only common sense to do so.

"Hey, that must be lies they say about you being mean," said the billy goat.

"Yeah. I really love animals," I said. "You can go now, if you want to," and I went back under the bridge.

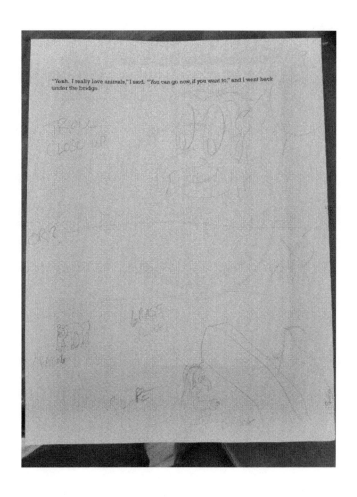

Then I heard wheels. It was the teenage Gruff on a skateboard.

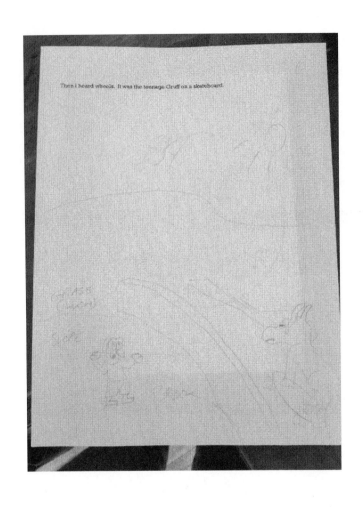

He hit a rock and went flying over the side of the bridge.

I had to help him out of the water. I don't think he was a very good swimmer.

The oldest billy goat saw me and he thought I was trying to drown his little brother.

He rammed me at least 30 feet!

Now look at me. I'm in the hospital with a broken arm and leg.

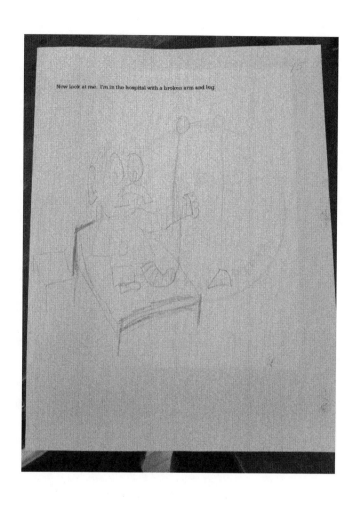

Epilogue (Don't Be Sad)

Rejected

Scarlett places the book back on the shelf, saying, "I don't think I want to read about a dirty bird."

"Seen enough already, am I right?"

"Don't even start," Scarlett replies to her friend. "What do you have there?"

"It's *Björk as a book*. I think it's from back when *Vespertine* was released. It looks super!"

"Does anyone still listen to Björk?"

"Who cares? I think she's hot."

Mercanary appreciates that Björk is just too good for our world.

"Really?"

"Very." She playfully swoons, holding the book to her breast.

"You don't think she's appropriating your culture? Like, using all that geisha, neo-Tokyo stuff?"

"Uhhhm. No. Not at all." She turns, moving for the cash queue.

"But, she's clearly not Japanese."

"No." She laughs, as the pair step in line. "Does it bother you?"

Scarlett fidgets a little, and she responds, "I dunno. Some people get upset about this sort of thing. I was just trying to be sensitive about it."

"Scarlett, do you think Japanese people get their panties twisted about gaijin celebrating our culture? Like, are we telling people they can't make believe they're ninja or they can't write haiku?"

"Well, no. I guess not."

"Yeah. Not everyone is offended by these things. It's okay. You look uncomfortable."

Scarlett's nervous, like when one loses their cool façade in the middle of a first date.

> Mercanary appreciates the horror of such epiphanies.

"No. You're right. I'll drop it."

"Yes. Relax!" She smiles at Scarlett and purchases the book from Mr. Manse, and he places it in a paper bag for her, smoothes the creases, and seals the top with a sticker, as per her usual preference.

The two women leave the House of Broken Books and walk up the alleyway's stairs without any rush to return to work.

"This is where I go right."

"Yeah, and I go left. Lunch hours are never long enough."

"I know," she replies, watching Scarlett stretch her arms as they breach the peak of the stairs to the sidewalk on Duckworth. "Will I see you again before SongzYaWanna?"

"I dunno. I have a bunch of split shifts scheduled."

"That sucks."

"Yeah," Scarlett says with a tinge of exhaustion. "We're having a little gathering for my new roommate on Friday. He's an old friend. You should come by."

"Friday? I'm working on a project. If we're finished early, ma-a-a-a-a-a-aybe."

"Okay. If you can't come, let's try to meet for lunch again next week."

"I'd like that." She smiles at Scarlett, admiring her hair in the breeze.

"Same. Today was nice."

"It still is!"

"Yes." Scarlett hugs her friend. They share a tender squish, and she continues, "You're right. I'll be in touch, Rei!"

"I hope you will," Rei replies with a wink, and the two part ways.

Rei skips three steps, arms swinging, and then calms herself to a perky walk. She hugs her new book and lets out a hopeful sigh as Harry crosses her path.

He turns. She's petite and cute, wearing a white tank that exposes her waist, jeans torn at the ass cheeks, and a yellow-and-black flannel shirt tied to hang on her left, ensuring a good peek from the rear.

Fuck, Harry thinks, she's hot.

He steps up to the entrance of Wiggly's Fin-n-Feather and pauses.

Rei unlocks the entrance to Magritte's Gallery and Studio, which is adjacent to Wiggly's storefront on the street.

Mercanary appreciates there are hearts bound up in art. Mercanary also appreciates that each time Del raps "for us," one can choose to hear "for Russ."

She gives Harry a sly grin.

He brightens and nods in response.

Mercanary sways his hips and tail, his beak

agape.

This isn't their first exchange, but neither has spoken to the other, and Harry's been working at Wiggly's for three weeks now.

"Whatcha standin' around gawkin' at?" A frazzled voice hollers through the kitchen window at Harry. It's Roz, the manager, the taskmaster.

"It's a beautiful day. I'm just taking in the view. Might try it once in a while, Roz."

"I've got enough to view back here." She gestures with disgust at the stack of orders awaiting delivery. "You got to show up on time for the lunch rush, ya know."

Mercanary swoops into the kitchen, rising up behind Roz and blowing raspberries over each of her shoulders.

"I'm on time. My shift doesn't start for another 3 minutes." Harry points to the clock above the register. Mercanary folds his wings in defiance and leans up against the freezer.

"Hrmph," Roz snorts, and then she wipes her nose in her sleeve. "Just get these orders out. This whole stack goes to Specific Place."

"Yeah, I know. These are the regulars – law offices, security staff. I know the routine."

"Yis now! Knows the routine, do ya? Been 'ere a week and 'e knows the routine." Roz elbows

Spence in the ribs, her way of intimidating a laugh out of the cook. He laughs, but his tone is unconcerned.

"I'm catching on. Gimme a break, Roz. This is my third week now."

"You gotta work before you gets a break, b'y. Wha' d'ya t'ink dis is? Pac-Man's day off? Git to it!"

Harry removes his backpack, placing it in his tiny locker, and he packs the orders into the food carrier, checking each address as he loads the bag. Mercanary pretends to take notes on an invisible pad.

"Right. Well, I'm on the clock starting now, so I'm outta here."

Harry's lucky he doesn't spend much of his time in Wiggly's with this crowd. He'd've lost his patience on the second day. He'd've quit already, but Bob really pulled through with this gig when Harry really needed it, and Harry's appreciative. So, this is it for now.

Harry doesn't drive to make the lunch rush deliveries. Specific Place is just a few blocks away on Water Street, so he lugs the orders there on foot, takes the elevator to the top, and makes deliveries to different office suites as he takes the stairs back down.

The lawyers he serves here don't tip him ever,

but the security guards tip well. The paralegals and articling students almost never order anything. They tend to brown-bag their lunches.

Mercanary appreciates this.

Harry's been eating fries with fish or chicken each shift. It's an unwritten perk of the job. According to Spence, you get a meal for each shift. Harry's not too keen on eating the same old thing each day for weeks, but he knows better than to turn away a meal he's worked for. For some undiscussed reason, Mercanary hasn't gotten upset about Harry's diet. Harry's happy enough about that.

After taking care of the lunch rush, Harry returns to Wiggly's, fends off Roz's nagging, and drives out the other orders as they're readied. Ending his shift after 11 and reeking of fryer fat, Harry drives home for the night.

The 323 has been holding up alright. Harry's had to replace the struts and transmission since moving back to St. John's, but he feels sporadic repairs are better than lease payments on a new vehicle. The 323 keeps him mobile when it's not in the shop. It's still good.

He pulls into the driveway on Neverland, parking between a Camaro and an Impreza. His roomies own those, and he can only dream of such. No one ever parks in the townhouse's garage.

"Hey, hey! I'm home," Harry calls out as he enters on the ground floor. Mercanary follows closely behind him.

"I'm just finishing up an article," a deep voice hollers from the third floor. "I'll be done in a few minutes. Let's have a smoke!"

"You got it, Max! I'll twist one now."

Harry doesn't go up the stairs. His room is on the ground floor, behind the garage door. He was warned of this before he took the room, but a room without a window is just the sort of thing Harry needs. Plus, the converted garage is huge for a bedroom, so it's almost as if he's on his own down here. He throws his backpack onto his loveseat, changes out of his greasy clothes, and rolls a joint on top of his highboy.

Mercanary appreciates those who rise up as well as Canadian content.

He climbs the stairs to the second floor, which is level with the backyard, and he plops onto the couch beside Max. The shower is running on the third floor.

"Light 'er up," she says, tossing a newspaper onto the coffeetable.

Maxine Goldman's an editor for *The Overpass*, a local arts and culture paper. On the other hand, Maxine Nasty is a dom. She has an imposing presence in any role, but Max is chill. That is, unless something else is called for. That's how Harry's room became vacant a month ago.

Harry sparks up, inhales, and passes to Max, asking as he exhales, "What're you workin' on?"

"Nothing interesting," Max says, sounding drained. "It's another piece about the bloody construction of that damned dam. I'm getting sick of it all. It's the same old story with every megaproject."

"Yeah. Ain't that the truth."

"I need to get back into the arts writing, but I never have time. There's too much on my plate editing this paper. I never have time to write what I want to write anymore."

"Yeah, but now you're the boss."

"I've always been the boss." She's not referring to her job, and she passes the joint.

"True enough."

Mercanary flies up over the stairs, and then he curls up silently near Harry's feet, nuzzling his beak into Harry's heels.

"Harry. I like you. You've got class."

"Stop that," Harry says to Mercanary and then continues his conversation with Max, "Oh, you hardly know me yet."

"I think I've seen enough to know."

Mercanary looks up at Harry, eyes full of joy.

"I don't know about that."

"You writing anything now?"

"I'm working on a short story. I dunno. Maybe it could be a serial or something."

"Harry, start low and go slow," she advises. "If no one knows you as an author, then no one wants to hear about your ideas for a series."

"Yeah?" He's not hurt. Harry respects her experience.

Mercanary appreciates a good Mer-Man while also having compassion for those who try.

Upstairs, the shower shuts off.

"Look, if you're an emerging writer in the scene, be modest. Pitch that as a short story. Forget anything like a series. I mean, forget it until you've established yourself."

"Yeah," Harry agrees. "That makes sense. You need people to know your name first, and then you might have success pitching something like a series."

"Exactly. See? You're quick."

"Ha! You just taught me that. I'm not that quick."

"If you can listen to advice and consider it, then you're one step ahead of some of the writers I have

128

to work with. And I say you're quick."

"Thanks, Max. That means a lot."

"You could be hot, too. Give yourself a chance, Harry."

Only hearing that Harry is hot, Mercanary rolls over onto his back, lifts his tail into the air, and begins fanning Harry and Max.

"Is the deck door left open?" Max asks. "She always leaves it open in the evenings, but – the flies. Ugh! I'm always telling her to keep it closed. Be a doll, and close it."

Harry complies, dousing the roach in the ashtray, and then walking out through the kitchen and dining room. Mercanary follows. The deck door is closed. Harry knew it would be, but the mail's always left on the dining room's table.

He sifts through it and finds a thick, wrinkled, and thoroughly taped envelope addressed to him. It's from his folks. He finds no letter from them inside. This is just mail forwarded from home, an envelope of envelopes. Most are promotional junk mailings, some are from the government, and then Harry finds four from publishers.

Mercanary peeps over Harry's shoulder and the two eagerly rip one open.

"We regret to inform you that your story does not conform with our submission guidelines.

Hence, you have been disqualified from consideration."

Harry's not upset. He knows a writer must face rejection. Mercanary remains hopeful, and Harry tears into the second.

"Thank you for your submission. We are not interested in children's stories at this time."

Mercanary looks to Harry for his reaction. Harry's still in good spirits. They open the third.

"Ebb and Flow Press thanks you for sending these notes about *The True Story of the Three Billy Goats Gruff*, but it is unclear how this is a true story in any sense, and we can't imagine how such a book would fit in with our existing catalogue."

Mercanary reads Harry's reaction. Harry remains positive. He places the third rejection letter on the table with the first two, he takes a deep breath to build suspense, and then he rips open the final one.

"Ingeinus Books thanks you for your interest, but *Lace Pinkertons* isn't a project that we're interested in at this time."

Harry reads that again.

Mercanary looks puzzled.

Harry reads it again.

"What the fuck is this?!?"

Mercanary shrugs his wings.

"Dude, that's not even my story."

Mercanary shrugs.

"Did they even read my pitch?"

Mercanary shrugs.

"Did they misspell their own name?"

Mercanary shrugs.

"How will I ever get published if they aren't even going to read my pitch?"

"Chirp. Chirp. Coo, coo. Chirp!" Mercanary exclaims as he performs a complex sequence of gestures.

Harry understands the scheme.

"Yeah. That might actually work, ya know?"

"CHIRP!"

Mercanary appreciates an apt chimaera.

Harry throws the rejection letters in the trash as the two return to the living room.

Scarlett's on the couch with Max. She's drying her hair with a towel and venting to Max about the guests at the Omega.

"Hey, Harry!"

"S'up, Scarlett?"

"Nada. Excited for Friday?"

131

"You know it. Can't wait!"

"Super! I'm really looking forward to it. It's been too long." She can't help but make a sideways glance at Max.

"That's not my fault," Max interjects instantly.

"I didn't say it was, Max," Scarlett replies.

"Toni could've cleared her things out sooner. It's not like I could make her do it any quicker."

"I know, Max. We get it. It's alright. No one's blaming you."

Harry never speaks up when they talk about this. He's just happy to be here. He imagines it must've been a rough split between Toni and Max, and Scarlett probably witnessed most of it.

Scarlett continues, speaking more to Harry again, "Look, this won't be a super wild party –"

"But, I am a wild party," Harry quips.

Mercanary rolls on the floor.

"Ha! Yes! Kim Mitchell." Max brightens at the reference.

"– because we're moving on from those parties. This should be more subdued, more adult."

"Best kind," Harry assures her. "Keep it tame. Gotcha."

"Keep it classy," Max adds, winking at Harry.

The rest of the work week passes normally without much disruption. Harry is even more familiar with his routine, and he's become more efficient at avoiding Roz's badgering. He doesn't bump into the gallery worker outside Wiggly's, though he would've liked that.

Mercanary keeps Harry company day and night. The mythical bird-fish floats near his human all over town, causing harmless mischief with each delivery. Since Harry quit puppeteering, the two have been inseparable, and Harry's generally in good spirits.

With Mercanary at his side, he even submits a draft of his story to *Hardcore Dungeons*, an online literary magazine with quarterly releases. They feature science-fiction and fantasy works and cater to the current epoch of digital pulp fiction readers. E-books for a buck. That's their model. Contributors are paid, but it's a flat rate upfront with no residuals. Harry gets it. Start low and go slow, and so he emails his pitch, resume, and manuscript to their editors on Tuesday. Harry feels accomplished as soon as he hits send, so Friday evening's bound to be a good time.

We'll see about that.

Harry worked the early shift, so he's fresh and clean by 9. He splashes Old Spice on his waist and chest, rubbing the musk into his groin and across his chest. He pulls on his jeans and a shirt that he only buttons up halfway. It's summer. He's hot, and he's all set to entertain. He grabs his half-empty pint of homebrew and goes upstairs.

Scarlett's flipping through their combined record collection, chatting with her friends, and she places a black circle on the turntable. The Cat Empire plays. It's "Hello, hello." Max shrieks from upstairs when she recognizes it, and then she rumbles down the stairs, wine spilling all over. She points at Scarlett, and the two bounce out their routine.

Things go well.

Vince and Patti come by. Vince has no trouble schmoozing, and Patti's in her zone here, too. She tells Harry about the new band, Tanx Grrlz. They've only played a couple of shows so far, but now they're going to start wearing animal masks all the time. Patti's got an owl's head to wear for their next gig. Harry tells her this sounds awesome and that Max would be stoked to hear about it, too. Then, Harry starts up a conversation with Vince about teaching literature. He knows Vince can gush on endlessly about the art of a plot and how to compose concise prose, and Harry picks up a lot from him like this.

Later, Bob and Marg drop in. Marg's already had a few, and she's as chatty and grabby as ever. She greets Harry with a hug and an arse squeeze. Bob doesn't mind.

"Brother, you've got to watch out when she gets a hold of you like dis. She has a firm grip." Bob laughs a full-bellied haw-haw and a tinge of his French accent pokes through.

Bob Barthes' a large man and in great shape. This gives him a confidence that Marg could grab any ass and still come back for his. It's not a bad thing. They reciprocate each other's energies like this.

"I'm stoked to see you two. I didn't know if you'd be in town."

"I just got back. I had to –"

"You had to see a man about a horse. Yeah, man. I get it. You don't have to explain."

Mercanary appreciates wonderlust as well as wanderlust.

"Thanks, Harry" Bob replies. "Here, wait until you see what I have here for you, my man."

"Whatcha got?"

"My man, the man of the hour, the reason for our being here tonight..."

"What? What is it?"

Bob reaches into his arse pocket, takes out his wallet, opens it, removes a folded comic book page, wraps his other arm around Harry's shoulder, pulls his friend closer, and, revealing its contents, whispers in his ear, "Scooby snacks."

135

"Dude, you know me! LSD!"

"Indeed! Welcome back, brother! Now, these are potent. I'd only drop a half, know wha' 'm sayin'?"

"Right. I'll drop two tonight."

"You sick, man. Sick." Bob laughes and laughes and laughes.

Harry licks the tip of his index finger, dabs a blotted square, not two, and places it under his tongue.

"I'll be right behind you. Got a knife? Scissors? I intend to stick to a half."

Bob keeps the comics page folded in his palm. The two retrieve a knife from the kitchen, Bob takes half a hit, gives the other half to Marg, and then they mingle before it kicks in.

The next half hour or so goes splendidly.

Scarlett's getting along with Vince, Bob, and Marg. Although none of them have really hung out much since she left university to do hospitality at the college, everyone keeps in touch with Bob, and that's how he learned she had a room. Max and Patti get along great. They bond over their mutual love of Hewlett's Gorillaz, and then Max invites Patti for a joint and to view *La Belle Époque* with some friends in her room on the third. Harry follows them upstairs, drains his bladder in the toilet, checks himself in the mirror – not melting yet – and descends too quickly to the second floor.

He notices his dizziness at the top of the stairs to the entrance on the ground floor. He pauses, clutching at the handrail.

R
  e
    a
     l
      i
       t
        y

            s
              l
                i
                  d
                    e
                      s.

A bell rings.

He doesn't respond. His vision's all snowy with blinking stars.

A bell rings.

137

His vision returns as the dizziness melts away like a film on fire.

He looks down.

Mercanary appreciates unsigned artists almost as much as he appreciates cultural heritage. Mercanary also appreciates such golden opportunities.

A petite figure closes the front door. It's a she. She's a she. She's wearing a white dress. Is she a swan? No. It's green. She's wearing a green top and jeans. No. She's nude. Her skin's green. There are seven of her. She sprouts wings. They each sprout wings, sparkling and translucent green. Seven nude green faeries.

It's kicking in now, for sure.

And then she's in his face.

She's not green. Her hair is styled in a dark bob, her skin is as pale as fallen snow, eyeliner extends from her eyes reaching for her earlobes, her lips are matte black, and her cheeks are red with blush. Is it make-up? Is she flushed? Harry thinks she looks like a punk rock geisha. Who *is* she?

"I know you," she says.

Harry responds, "That's reassuring. How do – "

"Rei!" Scarlet calls out from behind Harry, seeing her friend from out in the kitchen. She puts down her martini and rushes to greet Rei.

Harry stands back, just a little off balance.

One word repeats in his mind, layered over and over, like some kind of echo, so that – in an instant – resounds the name Rae.

"Scarlett!"

"Rei! You made it!"

"I did! I'm right here."

"Come in! Let me make you a drink."

"I brought absinthe."

The two women take no notice of Harry's stupor. He's still standing upright. He's still good. He's still good, even if it feels like his face is melting.

Mercanary appreciates there is room to exhibit diversity in the arts.

When Harry wanders through the kitchen, Rei is setting a sugar cube ablaze on top of a glass of smoky green elixir. Scarlett's impressed at the ritual of it all. Rei says something about not caring about the particulars as Harry stumbles into the dining room and out onto the deck in the back. Bob's there having a cigarette.

"Dude, I'm getting tracers. You see this?" Bob writes in the air with the ember as his ink.

"Ye-e-e-e-e-eah," Harry utters. "Did you just write me a poem?"

139

"No, Harry. That's my name."

"What? My name's Harry."

"Yes, Harry. You're Harry. I'm Bob."

"Rae?"

"Aww, fuck," Bob's sober enough to know Harry's not going to have anything like a good time if he gets his mind stuck in the mud like this. He tries to lift him out of the mire. "Nah, brother. I'm Bob. You're Harry. You got this. I gave it to you. Come here. Smoke this."

Harry takes Bob's lit cigarette and smokes it.

"Fill your lungs," Bob instructs. "In deep! Take it in!" He takes a deep breath as an example, a demonstration Harry follows. "And breathe fire, my dragon, my friend!"

Harry exhales the tobacco smoke. It billows and swirls and dances, and it comes from inside him. He's delighted, and he's been sufficiently distracted.

Bob and Harry share another cigarette after that one's out. Harry tells Bob about working at Wiggly's. Bob knew Roz was a bit of a hardass, and then he tells Harry that he has another courier gig lined up for him. Harry's unable to keep track of the details, but he nods and goes along with each of Bob's prompts before going back inside.

Scarlett's dancing with her friends in the living

140

room. Rei's dancing too, and Harry joins, dancing aimlessly with everyone and avoiding eye contact.

He's not dancing long when he tells Scarlett he's full of acid and in need of a long walk. She understands. It's a part of the rhythm of it all.

Harry excuses himself from the dancers, and Scarlett and Rei each smile in parting. He doesn't bother to find Vince and Patti. They're upstairs. He'll see Max again in the morning. He waves goodnight to Bob and Marg in the kitchen, and then he's out.

A long walk is exactly what Harry needs, and it doesn't feel like a long walk at all, not when one's fuelled by acid. He has that special bounce in his step, even if his mind's locked in on difficult memories. From Neverland, Harry walks down Thorburn past one mall and onto Columbus, and then down Columbus and past another mall until he finds himself at Bowring Park.

It's after 3. He finally takes a seat on the stone wall surrounding the Peter Pan statue.

This is where he and Rae had their final fight.

He's reliving it as he studies the animals that dance and frolick, thriving off Pan's perpetually youthful aura.

Mercanary swings his head up over Pan's shoulder, surprising Harry.

141

Mercanary appreciates such moments to reflect.
Mercanary also appreciates which side of the
looking glass is which.

Harry hadn't noticed his mystical companion following him here, and that's just when Harry feels a vibration in his pants.

He checks his phone.

Harry's missed messages from Vince and Patti. They're just saying they had fun.

But there's a message from a number he doesn't recognize. He taps it.

"Harry? Tom Wise from *Hardcore Dungeons*. We want to include your story in our next issue. We'll include it as-is, so we can make the deadline. How's 50 bucks sound?"

Harry looks up at Mercanary. Mercanary's smile broadens, and he radiates glee as he returns Harry's gaze.

Harry's not tripping nearly as much as when he was peaking, but he still can't believe his eyes. His thoughts race round and round, like a turntable overcharged to spin at 60 revolutions per minute.

Mercanary rests a calming wing across Harry's shoulders.

"I'm going to be a published writer."

Individual Duality

A critic says:
"It is nothing,
A throw-away.

"It is a poem.

"It is thought,
Written,
Spoken,
And gone."

A poet responds:
"Aren't we all?"

Da Pipe Track

Comin' straight off da Pipe Track
Crazy muthafucka davaflava
And I'm actin' with that ill behaviour

What's that?
I never claimed to be a saviour
What's that?
Come again, I'll have to h'ave ya

In Refuge

"Showdown at the Cactus's Prick"

"The Way of War is a Way of Deception."
– Sun-tzu

"When you are even with an opponent,
it is essential to keep thinking of
stabbing him in the face...."
– Miyamoto Musashi

Far from Shoukyoku's Imperial City, a troop of
eight armed soldiers ride west along a twisting trail
through a hilly region of a large coniferous forest.
Industry has not yet spread out to these lands, but
the Emperor demands assimilation. The trees here
are tall and sparse, and although this lonely trail
leads to the farthest reaches of Emperor
Shoukyoku's domain, the Imperial banner
nevertheless flies at regular intervals, posted every
thousand paces on the roadside. These royal blue

banners bear Emperor Shoukyoku's coat of arms, a sitting golden tiger with red stripes and a red troll's face. The flags mark the land as Shoukyoku's possession; they are a persistent reminder to travellers on the road, but they also appear intermittently and without warning throughout the wilderness, reinforcing the Emperor's omnipresence. The soldiers, too, are easily recognizable as the property of Emperor Shoukyoku. Their leather-band armour is dyed red and their conical, woven helms feature a prominent golden troll-tiger with exaggerated horns. As if it weren't enough, every troop of the Imperial Legion must include a standard bearer, yet again reinforcing this overbearing motif. The whirring of the roadside flags as the soldiers speed past creates an odd rhythm mingled with the cacophony of thunderous horse hooves pounding the ground.

The forest begins to thin as the soldiers near the limit of Shoukyoku's influence. Beyond, the land is barren, a desert that's been left mainly deserted. The sky is open, nearly cloudless, revealing an endless canopy of hazy red, as if the Emperor had made the very heavens his banner. The sun blazes, the air is hot and the land is dry. The soil is cooked and it begins to crack under the heat. Life struggles in this land. Shrubbery is scattered and few, but cactus plants manage to survive in the oppressive heat. Shoukyoku's banners do not stretch out through this land, not yet. Indentured labourers and criminals have been brought out to expand the empire. Taskmasters ensure productivity remains optimal, and the workers continue planting flags in the dirt, daring to venture no further than the reach of a longbow from the treeline. Some curse the soldiers under their breath as they ride towards a narrow canyon not far in the distance.

This wasteland is known as Tynet. It is a vast land, harsh and inhospitable. Dissidents, outlaws, and criminals from the surrounding sovereignties frequently find refuge here simply because the authorities would rather not maintain pursuit through such a foreboding landscape. One such refuge is Runner's Rest, a tiny pit stop consisting of a few hobbled shanties hidden in the crevice beneath a large crag in the cliffside of a narrow canyon, located not far from the Shoukyoku border. A small river trickles through the bottom of the ravine. Starving trout jump after the flies that float above the stillest pools, the same pools providing potable water for the grimy tavern's stills. A filthy sign reading "The Cactus's Prick" hangs half-off the hinges above the door, which is merely a moth-eaten horse blanket tossed over the entrance. A scrawny old nanny goat is tied to a hitch outside and some chickens can be heard clucking around the side of the saloon. The tavern is at least three stories tall. Built from straw, timber, and a pale orange clay, the Cactus's Prick is moulded into the cliffside and features a mishmash of tiny hovels with bedrolls, making the tavern a nearly adequate hostel. Inside, a slight, young

146

woman with dark hair and fair skin serves a table of three ruffians small glasses of potent liquor, while the potbellied man behind the bar brims widely at the sight of the lonesome hermit's custom.

"MWA-HAA!" the bartender wails. "I've not seen Imperial coin since my little Moonshine suckled at the teats of whores!" The woman's jaw drops and she shoots the old man a quick glare that soon breaks into a smile, expressing the love of a daughter for her father. The toughs laugh loudly and poke at the girl, but she deftly escapes their playful striking, returning behind the bar with her father.

"You'll see far less of it, too, Fat Pint, once they've taken this land from you," the lonesome hermit replies bitterly, loud enough for the rowdy patrons to notice. The hermit's bearing is wild, but he maintains a keen wit. His tanned skin betrays a life of hunting and foraging under the scorching sun. The hermit carries with him a long, straight walking stick, and although the wood is knotted, it is a sturdy staff. His clothes are made of loose linen, scraps, patches, furs and worn leather bands. While his beard is patchy and rough, his hair is kempt and mostly hidden under his conical, woven helm. This helm is peculiar in that where there would typically be a family crest, his bears an improvised emblem resembling a bird-fish chimaera, a wondrous creature that can only be seen as a mercanary. He carries a large satchel with

147

a number of drinking gourds hanging from the strap. What marks the hermit as unique, however, is that he is not only armed with a longbow and quiver but he wears a weathered daisho as well, the longsword and shortsword of noble warriors known respectively as katana and wakizashi. "I'll tell you again, Shoukyoku's Imperial Legion will not be far behind those peons planting flags along the forest's edge," he continues. "Perhaps the Emperor will force you to plant flags yourself, if he does not feed you to his dogs."

"BAH! Hermit, you've been holed up in your cave far too long," the robust bartender retorts. "Since you first laid eyes on those flag-planting peons, you've got it into your head that Shoukyoku is about to invade the vast and empty desert. Twice this week already you've come down here to spout these prophecies of our doom, but there are no soldiers demanding our surrender. And last month, too, you warned us all the same. But what could the Emperor ever want with what little we have? There is nothing but dust and beggars in Tynet!" Eyeing the current patrons of the Cactus's Prick, he rubs clean one of his infamous larger pint glasses with a grubby, dry cloth. Then he spits air at it to demonstrate the strength of his position, making an exaggerated *pah-tooh* sound as he does so. The proprietor is quite proud of himself for his moment of wisdom, and his beaming smile betrays his joviality.

"Be fair, Fat Pint," one of the ruffians slyly

adds, "we do not come here begging for your coin."

"If only you were begging for coin," Fat Pint replies sharply. "No. Instead you come here begging for more wine or another round of mescal! You come begging for one of our finest beds to rest your tired, penniless arse in!"

"Yes," interjects one of the sharp-witted ruffians, turning his lecherous gaze to the nubile young Moonshine, "the bed she's in!" The ruffians let out a roar of laughter, while Moonshine shakes her head. Moonshine is no pushover; she knows full well that if she acts coyly with the customers, they are more likely to leave her a nice tip. That is, if they even have anything of value. By the look of it, these men don't.

"Or you come here begging for a quick romp with my little Moonshine, you filthy buggers," Fat Pint acknowledges regretfully. He resents the men who make vulgar advances towards his daughter, but he knows she's coming of age. He only wishes she could find herself a man who would provide for her and keep her safe, but the chance of finding a man like that in Runner's Rest is unimaginable. He forgets she needs no man to take care of her.

As the awkward laughing passes, the hermit glares quietly at the others for a short moment before resuming his appeal.

"Enjoy your laughter now, for when those flags flood this land, there will be none here to stand up to the Imperial Legion," the hermit warns starkly.

149

"I plan to move further west. The land is barren, but it will provide me sustenance enough to reach the village of Redemption."

"BAH! Redemption is little more than a thieves den and a whore house," Fat Pint scoffs. "All you'll get there is the itch, hermit!"

"You should pack your things and leave, as well," the hermit calmly suggests, disregarding the barkeep's jest. "You've had far too few patrons in recent months; even the regular squatters of Runner's Rest have enjoyed their rest but have returned to running," he reasons. Fat Pint, Moonshine and the others listen and feign indignation, but each of them realize there is some truth to the hermit's words. The hermit lets the truth of his words sink in for a moment, then he continues, "Shoukyoku either thinks there is something of value in this land or his greed now covets even the poor man's dirt. I'm telling you, it is time to – "

The hermit abruptly cuts his plea short. His ears perk up, and then he jerks his head to better discern some distant sound. The others seem puzzled by his quick change in demeanour, but after a moment they also hear the sound of thunderous horse hooves pounding along the trail. Fat Pint and Moonshine look to each other in bewilderment while the ruffians seem confused, but the hermit is still listening. Then he turns quickly to face Fat Pint and Moonshine behind the bar, turning his back to the horse blanket covering the entrance and exclaiming loudly, "A round of your best mescal for my friends at the table, Moonshine!" The ruffians cheer at the prospect of free booze. "And, Fat Pint, I would like one of your famous large pints. Give me your strongest liquor." Moonshine and Fat Pint stir from their daze and fall into the more natural motions of serving the order.

Beyond the fabric door, they can hear the horses have slowed from a gallop to a soft trot and, finally, to a halt. The horses neigh and snort. A stern voice outside the Cactus's Prick issues what sound like orders, and a number of men dismount. Inside the tiny tavern, Fat Pint and Moonshine pour up stiff drinks, the ruffians eagerly await those drinks, and the hermit sits with his back to the door. He hears four men approach the entrance. One whips the fabric door open and the warm breeze wafts the rising dust cloud into the small hovel of a drinking hole. Standing in the doorway, the man is a tall and dark silhouette, outlined by the bright orange rays of the sun beaming into the canyon that hides Runner's Rest. His profile is intimidating; his figure is like that of a horned demon. He stands rigid, taking in an account of the premises. Moonshine delivers a round of mescal to the toughs sitting at the table. Fat Pint serves the hermit a large pint of barely drinkable, high-proof alcohol, then he turns to the shade in the door, offering a half-hearted greeting, "Welcome to the Cactus's Prick, stranger. Our liquor has enough kick to strip the paint off the Holy Temple's walls. If you're here to drink, come in and keep that blanket closed...." Fat Pint's speech trails off as the dark figure steps fully into the hovel, followed by three other men, each clad in the stark armour of the Imperial Legion, one holding the royal blue standard with the sitting troll-tiger.

The first soldier to enter steps boldly to the centre of the room, his countenance marks him as an officer but the prostate posturing of the page beside him bearing the Imperial standard confirms his rank. Two other foot soldiers file in behind the officer and page. The officer sizes up the room, eyeing the ruffians, Moonshine, Fat Pint, and the back of the hermit, who has not turned to watch their grand entrance. The officer sighs with annoyance, then whines sardonically, "Oh, my. I would never have expected to see dogs living in this plague-infested den, nevermind the rats we find here."

The soldiers laugh, the young page almost whinnies like a horse, but the locals are unimpressed. Moonshine continues picking up empty flagons from the toughs' table. The toughs, meanwhile, eye each other, trying to gauge how drunk or courageous the other feels. The hermit still has his back to the soldiers when Fat Pint asks "Are you fine foreign soldiers here to drink or just to take in the sights?"

"Quiet! You are a fat failure of a man, heathen," the officer spits the words like venom from his mouth, then he continues, clearing his throat and regaining his superior attitude. "By the divine grace and benevolence of the sagacious Emperor Shoukyoku, you are given this opportunity to repent your past lives as sinners and swear your fealty to the will of Shoukyoku, the Emperor, and His Most Sovergein State." The officer pauses here, as he fancies from time to time, to savour the reaction from potential converts. Fat Pint and Moonshine share a concerned glance. The ruffians are drunk, still drinking even, but they aren't equipped to fight armed and sober soldiers. None of them dare act against these pompous emissaries of the Imperial Legion, yet the hermit remains seated on a stool at the bar, a large pint of potent alcohol in his hand, his back turned to the soldiers. The officer looks around at each of them, and he cries, "Enough with the silence, peasants! Do you swear your fealty, or do we cut you down like mowing grass? Hm?" Quickly growing frustrated at the sight of the hermit's back, with ire beaming through a failed attempt at poise, he adds, "And, what amazing audacity can a desert rat have to think himself unconcerned with the question at hand? Hm?"

The hermit merely nods, grinning, with his back still turned to the officer who begins to steam with fury. Just before it seems the officer's temper is about to boil over, his young page leaps to his side, whispering a matter of lengthy detail in his ear. The tall officer stoops uncomfortably to listen to

153

his page's urgent counsel. This secret intelligence brings a hideous smile to his face, and a glint of either lust or greed flashes in his eyes. The page writhes with pleasure, like a good dog awaiting his bone. He's almost giddy leaping back to his official position, no doubt anticipating future rewards and comforts. The officer calls out to the hermit again, "So, this is where you've been hiding. You look like a filthy mongrel, you know, Captain."

The hermit lifts his head, acknowledging the officer's claim. He grasps his large pint and slowly turns to face the soldiers, hugging his walking stick with a hooked elbow.

The officer inhales through his teeth, making a mocking, hissing hoot at the dishevelled look of the hermit. "You've fallen far in just four years," the officer says, relishing over such a fortuitous find on what was to be a routine razing. He sniffs in the hermit's general direction, turns his nose up and grimaces in disgust. "Your attire bears the remnants of Imperial Legion armour, although you deface your splendid helm with – with – what is that thing?"

"A mercanary," the hermit states.

"A mercanary?" The officer looks to his lackeys and chuckles. "Fitting, isn't it?"

Lackeys nod.

The officer returns his gaze to the hermit sitting peacefully at the bar, and he continues, "Listen, what betrays your identity even more is that your daisho is undoubtedly from a very noble lineage.

You were born to a life of luxury. I cannot believe that *you* – this embarrassment of a wildman, this sad excuse for a trapper – *you* were praised on high, as if *you* would become the next Warlord of His Imperial Legion."

Fat Pint and Moonshine are shocked to hear such a fantastic story about the man they have known only as the hermit, the lonely man who would visit Runner's Rest maybe once or twice each month to drink, eat, and trade herbs and furs. Although they always wondered about the story behind his pair of swords, the proprietors of the Cactus's Prick found it more amusing to invent their own stories explaining the swords, and they considered it far less rude than prying into the solitary man's affairs.

"Yes, I know who you are," the Imperial officer says, pausing for dramatic effect, causing his page to stifle his barely restrained glee. "I know your name, Suzuki Haruko Sabaku. I know you are called Sabaku the deserter. I know you were the very essence of the sparkle in your father's eye. I know the disgrace you brought to your family and how your father, Lord Suzuki, died from the dishonour you brought upon your house. I know you are a treasonous traitor to our benevolent Emperor. I know you were crippled by your uncle as you fled in shame into the forest and, so it would seem, into the desert beyond. Most believe you had succumb to guilt and threw yourself from a cliff, but it seems you're not so fortunate." The hermit leans heavily on his knotted staff, while the officer and page are exuberant at this sign that seems to confirm his physical hindrance. Fat Pint and Moonshine look astonished, not quite knowing how to react to the presence of the soldiers and their accusations against their acquaintance. The toughs look impressed at the hermit's credentials, the effects of the potent mescal blossoming, giving the ruffians a reinvigorated appetite for destruction. The infantry accompaniment awaits orders from their commanding officer, anticipating that they will be capturing the traitor alive, and the remaining soldiers can be heard rummaging about the other shacks outside the Cactus's Prick.

The hermit steps off his stool, bearing his weight on his sturdy walking stick. He achieves a shaky balance and scratches at his face through his scraggly facial hair. He grins widely, and speaks confidently, "I am Sabaku the deserter, and you will leave my friends and I here," gesturing to the ruffians enjoying the round of complimentary mescal, "to enjoy our drinks. I am an eccentric and a cripple, and the others here are of no significance to Shoukyoku. Return to your masters. Inform them that Runner's Rest is abandoned." The hermit, or rather Sabaku the deserter, raises his glass to the ruffians who join him in a little cheer.

The officer is more than perturbed at this unexpected counter offer. The outlying rabble near the farthest reaches of Shoukyoku's border typically won't dare to resist the Imperial Legion;

those few rebels who do stand up to fight are immediately crushed by the Empire. The officer expected resistance today, but prior to embarking on the menial task of converting a tiny thieves' den, he had resolved to simply sacking the tiny settlement and razing whatever remained of little value. The newly discovered prospect – that delivering Sabaku the deserter to the Emperor would land him a lucrative promotion to a comfortable position in the Imperial City – was too much for the officer to give up without a fight. "I cannot comply with your request, deserter," the officer snarls. "I will make you kneel before the seat of the Emperor in front of all to see! They will fill my lap with riches and parade me through the streets of the Imperial City!" The officer is lustfully committed to this vision of his immediate future, and speaks from his perceived position of power, "Your friends here shall not be slain for harbouring a traitor..."

"BAH! I am sure that must be good news," exclaims Fat Pint in confusion and relief.

"...they'll be placed in irons and live out their days in servitude at the work camps out east," the officer sentences them to a life of hard labour as slaves. "But you, Sabaku, I'm sure the Emperor will want to make an example of you, and I have my doubts you would survive his judgement. Guards! Seize the crippled traitor! I expect the rest of this rabble to struggle even less than the sick or elderly against the might of the Imperial Legion."

157

The two soldiers draw their swords and slowly converge on the smiling traitor, eager to exploit his weakness if he dares to resist. The hermit leans heavily on his knotted staff, maintaining a shaky balance. The toughs look worried at the prospect of servitude until death, but they remain seated. Fat Pint is behind the bar and takes a number of slow steps away from the hermit. The barkeep shares a look with his daughter and, with two blinks and a glance, he motions for her to move towards the front entrance. Moonshine's heart is racing; she can hear her pulse beating in her ears. Her face is flushed, and she shoots back the bottom of a glass of mescal and contemplates gulping back what's left in the pitcher as she slips through the shadows around the officer and page, avoiding their notice.

Sabaku the deserter leans heavily on his staff as the two soldiers approach him, swords drawn at the ready. "You're under arrest, traitor! Surrender, or we'll have to hurt you," one soldier commands as he manoeuvres to grab Sabaku, taking one hand from his sword.

At this, Sabaku strikes!

Deftly, he uses his staff to hold his body aloft as he kicks the soldier square in his chest with a series of bicycle kicks, landing comfortably on his feet, cradling his staff in his arm.

The other soldier advances drawing back to strike with his sword, but Sabaku bends backwards, stretching the staff over his shoulder, reaching out to strike his aggressor twice – the first strike planted firmly into the soldier's nose, breaking it, while the second strike is a calculated blow to the throat which sends the soldier flying backwards, tumbling over barstools until his backside hits the floor.

The first soldier has regained his footing after that series of firmly planted kicks and attempts charging Sabaku, screaming "AAAII-YEEEE!" His sword is raised above his head with two hands, and, as he charges forward, Sabaku effortlessly braces his staff by his foot and lets it fall forward. It falls into the centre of the oncoming soldier's abdomen, knocking him to his knees, breathless, and the staff makes a wooden clacking sound as it comes to rest on the floor.

The officer looks cheated. "You merely feigned injury, traitor! You are truly dishonourable," the officer's voice indicates that his confidence wavers. "Guards! Get in here," he screams to the guards outside and draws his sword, hoping to hold Sabaku at bay until his men arrive.

Sabaku draws his katana, bringing the hilt high near his ear with the blade pointing straight towards the officer's face. He holds the sword with a controlled ease. The blade is set to kill, but Sabaku is willing to negotiate, "You can still walk away. Take your lackeys, return home, and tell your masters this place was empty. You can live with that shame, and they will believe such a lie."

Standing alone, facing the fierce figure of Sabaku the deserter, the officer contemplates leaving now with his tender skin unblemished, but once four additional soldiers shuffle in through the blanketed doorway, his confidence returns. He looks to his page for support and can see that he's also dreaming of reaping the rewards that would come with Sabaku's capture. Fat Pint has managed to back himself into a corner behind the bar. Moonshine has her back to the wall near the entrance but is within a few steps from the page. The soldiers have filed into the bar, standing with the table of ruffians between them and their target. The officer feels a rush rise through him as he deems the odds are in his favour, and he leaps forward letting out a feeble cry, "Get the traitor, men! HIE-YAAH!" The tall officer charges forward with his sword raised high above his head.

In the second it takes for the officer to fly recklessly across the barroom floor, sword held aloft, a flurry of events take place. As the foot soldiers try to rush past the toughs drinking at the table, one suddenly stands up, feigning a stretch and an exaggerated yawn, tipping his stool in front of the crowd of soldiers, tripping the first so that the others stumble on top of him. The ruffians look at their friend who stood up, as if he had taken some momentous action. The standing tough looks to his seated friends, saying "Well, he did buy the last round." This turns the tide for the drunken ruffians, who take this opportunity to pounce, fists flying madly, onto the clumsy Imperial soldiers. These men are wanted for one crime or another in the surrounding lands, and each of them surely resent any representation of authority. Not only is releasing their aggression on soldiers who mean to arrest and enslave them a worthwhile act of self-preservation, it is also one of their most treasured pastimes. Meanwhile, as soon as the officer lets out his wail and breaks into a charge, Moonshine spots the young page draw a throwing dagger and pull it back. She could not tell whether it was aimed at her father or Sabaku, nevertheless she smashed a thick clay mescal pitcher across the page's head, sending him crashing to the floor. Proud of her accomplishment, Moonshine still recoils from the violence, slipping back into the shadows near the entrance. She looks to her father for direction, but he only stands in awe of the violence surrounding him. Although the Cactus's Prick has been the venue for innumerable barroom brawls, Fat Pint has never been confronted with the Imperial Legion threatening to make him a slave of Shoukyoku.

The sounds of shattering pottery and the erupting scuffle mingle with the tall officer's weak cry as he continues his charge, sword held high above his head. Sabaku maintains his stance, his sword's blade stretched out before him, aimed straight at the officer's face. From the officer's perspective, he cannot accurately judge the length of the blade before him. He is slightly distracted by this, failing to notice the exposed timber ceiling beams. As he charges forward, he lunges to make a

161

lethal strike against the patient deserter. Sabaku stands ready to strike as the officer's sword hacks into the timber beam above his head. Sabaku takes a firm step forward and, with just a twitch of his sword's tip, he slices the officer from his chin to his brow, violently tearing through his flaring nostrils, knocking his troll-tiger helm to the floor. The officer lets out a cry of pain, and Sabaku steps back, adopting a more relaxed posture, lowering his sword so its tip floats just above the floor. The officer's helm clangs as it hits the dusty floor.

"My face! You cut my face," the officer cries. The toughs continue to beat on the prone soldiers. Moonshine still looks to Fat Pint for encouragement, direction, strength, anything, but she finds none in the face of the barkeep, who is still in shock just envisioning the repercussions that must follow assaulting an officer of the Imperial Legion.

"Leave and live, Imperial dogs," Sabaku the deserter issues this ultimatum, "or threaten us again and suffer the consequences."

The officer has his hands covering the wound on his face and blood spills from between his fingers. He takes his hands down, flicking blood from his hands onto the floor with a splatter. "Traitor," he says, "Sabaku the deserter." He pauses a second, reaching towards the hermit-warrior with one of his bloody hands. Then he abruptly shouts, "I'll still receive a parade for your corpse!" With those final words he snatches a dagger from his belt with his other hand, slashing wildly and lunging for Sabaku's throat. Sabaku must have anticipated the officer's aggressive intentions from the tone or rhythm of his voice because he merely twitches his wrist, angling his sword upwards, holding the hilt near his groin, so that the tip pierces the officer's chest as he blindly thrust at the so-called traitor. The blade punctures the officer's lung and he falls to the floor. Little clouds of dust blow out from around his body as it falls lifeless, merely dead weight.

Fat Pint stirs from his stupor only to realize there's a dead Imperial officer lying on the floor of the Cactus's Prick. His mind races with the horrors that they might suffer for this transgression against the Empire. The toughs ease up on the beaten soldiers, and the soldiers know to stay down. Moonshine begins cleaning up the shattered pitcher, not knowing what other action to take given the present circumstances. Sabaku stands still and stoic over his fallen opponent. As if returning from some distant place in his mind, Sabaku looks to Fat Pint and continues his earlier appeal, "I think now is the time to leave Runner's Rest."

The sky has grown much darker now, making unaided vision strained. They bind the six beaten soldiers and the unconscious page, then pile them into an old cart that Fat Pint has rigged to one of the soldier's horses. The page's standard is wedged between a mass of arms and legs so that it stands upright. The blood red banner with the sitting troll-tiger proclaims the "glory" of Shoukyoku's empire for all on the road to see. Sabaku slaps the horse and makes a clicking noise, and the horse begins to trot along the trail to make its way back to the Shoukyoku border, the old cart's wheels creaking as the horse climbs the path up the canyon's cliff.

Runner's Rest is no longer safe for these poor souls, and so they are forced to pack up whatever valuables they can carry only to venture out into the desert in search of somewhere safe to lodge. Since the soldiers won't be riding back to Shoukyoku, their horses are a welcome resource for this impromptu exodus. Moonshine is busy packing distillation equipment, vats, and tubing onto another cart, one already loaded down with some chickens in a small pen, clothes and blankets stuffed into every gap and crevice. She is lost in fancies, wondering what adventure she might find outside the canyon's walls. The toughs scour the other shacks of Runner's Rest, salvaging anything of value to trade in the next village. Fat Pint ties his old nanny goat to the cart so she can walk alongside it as they travel. He looks at the Cactus's Prick with sadness in his heart; it has been his home and livelihood for many years. Sabaku apologizes to the hospitable barkeep for bringing such bad fortune upon him and his fair daughter, but Fat Pint retorts soberly that he should not have been so blind to the Emperor's greed looming so closely on the horizon.

164

Sabaku sets out on foot, leaving another horse for Fat Pint and Moonshine to help trek their wares to another town. He plans to head further west through the desert wilderness to Redemption. He knows the town as a refuge for the more hardened outlaws and criminals who find their way to Tynet. He is not taken in by the hopeful name of this den of thieves, but he must go there if he wants to remain out of Shoukyoku's reach for long.

As Sabaku steps off the beaten trail and ventures forth into the cool desert night, elsewhere a horse hauls a cart of broken soldiers past a field of blood red banners. The horse-driven cart moves slowly closer to the eastern treeline, and a crew of beleaguered slaves look upon the sight in the flickering torchlight. Some of them laugh.

THE END
...perhaps not.

Declined

Saturday morning at their place on Neverland smells like scrambled eggs and sounds like a vegetarian vampire duck. Max is making breakfast in the kitchen while Vince and Patti sip coffee in the adjacent dining room. Bob and Marg are out back, smoking. They haven't tidied the blankets from the couch yet, but they flipped on an old VHS tape to cover the sighs coming from the shower upstairs. A plastic skeleton dressed as a cowboy sits alone in the recliner, the only eager voyeur.

Mercanary can count the reasons for hoarding toilet paper on one hand, too, but Mercanary doesn't even have hands. He must count using yours.

"I'm sorry to hear about all of that, Max. I hope she can still cover SongzYaWanna for *The Overpass*. I can't imagine how anyone would just abandon an offer like that."

166

"It's fully funded," Max adds, "so she'd be foolish not to go and just hand in any old article."

"Maybe she's nervous," Patti guesses. "SongzYaWanna is a trendy festival, right? Like, maybe she thinks she's not good enough – you know, as a journalist – to write the right piece."

"Lisa knows better than that," Max claims. "She knows I can edit anything into the right piece."

"Anxiety is a real thing, Max," Patti defends her speculation. "Stage fright. I get it. It's real."

"Patti makes a fair point, Max."

"I know she does," Max admits. "Fuck! I don't even want to think about it. It's Saturday. I'm putting on some bacon."

Max drops a pack of maple bacon into the frying pan, unseparated. Marg glides through the sliding deck door, followed by Bob. Upstairs, the shower shuts off, revealing muffled giggles.

Mercanary appreciates the appropriate use of screens to mediate contact.

"Breakfast sure smells sweet, Max," Bob assures her. "It's a real treat, eating someone else's food, ya know?"

"Thanks, hon!"

"Bob's a fiend for other people's cookin'," Marg adds.

"It's not like that," Bob says. "Our food is our food. You know I love it."

"Yis. I knows you loves it."

Patti looks to Vince with her eyebrow raised, but Vince is more accustomed to how this couple gets along, and he takes little notice of the tension that entered the dining room from the deck.

Footsteps prancing down the stairs herald Scarlett's entrance, and she's almost dancing into the kitchen when she sings, "Morning! Ooo, bacon!"

"There's loads for everyone," Max says with a smile. "Take a seat. I'll serve this up in a few minutes."

"Right," Scarlett says. "I'll just steep some tea."

Scarlett can't sit still, and she hops about the kitchen – dodging Max with each step – to make her tea. Bob excuses himself to tidy up the couch, Max flips sizzling bacon strips, and the others chat casually.

No one heard her coming and Bob had his back turned, but Rei pops her head in through the door to the kitchen long enough to say, "Okay, I've got to run. People to see. Art to do."

Scarlett skips over to her, grips Rei's hips, pulls her close, kisses her eagerly, and then says, "Text me your schedule, and we'll do this again."

"Sure. I'll see what I can do, babe." Rei's grin is coy, and Scarlett is excited. "I'll get in touch."

Rei slips from Scarlett's grasp, but their eyes remain locked until she takes the stairs to the front door. The rest return to small talk over breakfast and tea.

Rei's sitting on the bottom step lacing up her knee-high boots when Harry returns from his night of wandering.

"Hey," Harry greets her, "I know you."

She's quickly erect and in his face to reply with "You do."

That's when Rei tilts her head, swoons, and clasps Harry's cheeks in her hands.

She kisses him.

It's quick, but it's deep and wet and hot.

Harry kisses her back, and then she stops.

"I've got to run. I'll see you around, right?"

"Of course."

"Cool. Later!"

She leaves the door open behind her as she walks away.

Harry is stunned.

He watches from the door.

She looks back with a grin.

He smiles and closes the door.

What just happened?

Harry can't make sense of his good fortune, but he's happy enough to have it.

> Mercanary appreciates the potential of masks and games is often overlooked.

Joining his friends for breakfast, he tells them about his story being accepted by *Hardcore Dungeons*. He doesn't mention the kiss.

"That's wicked, Harry!" Max is genuinely proud of her roommate. She feels like he's her protégé, and this news gives her reason enough to take a chance on him. "Listen, *The Overpass* has a growing stack of review copies. Think you might want to review a few books for us?"

"For real, Max?"

"Yeah. It's not a paid gig, so it's not a big deal. You can keep the books you review, and it's writing experience. You know, beef up your street cred and all that."

"I get it," Harry replies. "Yeah, I can do that."

"Fuckin' right you can!" Max is stoked, like a mother watching her child take their first steps. "I brought a few home with me. You can take your pick. There's no deadline for these. Do whatever you can when you can."

"I'm on it, Max!"

And, Harry was on it that very afternoon as soon as their guests had gone.

Max's stack of books for review matches her tastes more than Harry's, but their interests overlap in the best places. His first choice is *Anarchy Revolution* by Sparky O'Ryan, PhD, a professor of folklore who had been one of the founding members of Newfoundland's first punk rock group, The Slims. The book is a hybrid memoir-manifesto, and it's just the sort of thing Harry loves to read.

He finishes reading it that night in between doing laundry.

Mercanary appreciates that one cannot walk in the light without one's shadow. Mercanary also appreciates clean laundry.

Sunday morning he writes the review. He takes the afterrnoon to edit his own work, and he hands a double-sided, printed page to Max before supper.

"Dude!" Max exclaims, adding flatly, "I'm going to need you to email me a document."

"Shit. Naturally. Will do."

Harry looks a little disappointed, and then Max takes the sheet from his hand. He smiles. She shakes her head. Mercanary draws a pair of machine guns from behind his back and fires a volley into the kitchen's ceiling, which is the floor of the third.

RA-TA-TA-TA-TA-TATATATATATAH!

"Holy fuck!"

Mercanary releases the triggers.

"Sheesh, it's not that big a deal, Harry."

The kitchen is unhurt.

Harry's surprised, but he shouldn't be. How can anything Mercanary does at this point be surprising, right?

Mercanary appreciates Johnny Rotten as well as the light side of life.

"Can I get another book from the stack?"

"Take 'em all if you want."

"I might."

He doesn't, though. He takes three more books to review for Max, leaving eight others behind. Without delay, he and Mercanary descend to his room, the dungeon, and he begins reading *Another Dory Story*, the sequel to the hit erotic thriller, *Dory Story*, by Frisky Driscoll.

Monday and Tuesday are mundane enough, but Wednesday's remarkable.

Harry's at Wiggly's packing up the orders for the lunch rush. Mercanary's enacting a puppet show across the back of the deep fryer with a chicken carcass and a fish fillet. On top of the regulars' orders for Specific Place, there's a large order for another firm to feed fifteen or more.

"Don't mess up that one, wizard boy," Roz hollers from across the counter, watching the new guy like he's about to rob the place. She calls Harry wizard boy now, as if learning the ropes was the height of his learned potential.

"I won't mess anything up, Roz," Harry claims with confidence, and that's when he notices the next order is from Rei.

His heart skips a beat and his cock gives a throb.

"Dude," he says to his friend, leaving a pause for suspense. "She knows I do these deliveries."

Mercanary nods eagerly, adding "Chirp!"

"She wants to see me."

"CHIRP, CHIRP!" Mercanary drops the food into the fryer.

"Specific Place can wait. I've got to see what this is all about."

"Coo?"

"It'll be fine. I'll do it right after."

Mercanary fluffs his plumage with an air of swagger as Harry closes his three fully loaded meal carriers. Spence returns to the kitchen from the employee's washroom, wiping his hands in a dish cloth.

"I didn't hear a flush," Harry says as he passes by the cook. Mercanary floats past overhead.

"I didn't hear anyone ask you," Spence mutters.

Harry just shakes his head, expelling the odor from his nostrils with a snort. He has more exciting events to explore in Magritte's Gallery and Studio next door.

The carriers are cumbersome, but Harry awkwardly enters the gallery with a gentle dingling signaling his presence.

No one's out front.

He lays the carriers down and quickly huffs his own breath in his palm. Mercanary passes him a mint, and Harry sucks it as he sizes up the showroom. It's clean and scentless and quiet. Paintings hang alongside photographs near sculptures placed on pedestals. There's a closed door to the back and a wire-framed spiral staircase leads to the second floor. A reception podium doubles as the point of sale, but it's unattended.

No one's in sight.

"Hey," Harry calls out. "Wiggly's is here! I've got just what you've ordered!"

"Bring it up," is the command heard from

above. "Just climb those stairs!"

Harry and Mercanary exchange a hopeful look, and then Harry takes Rei's order from the carrier and sprints for the stairs. Mercanary swoops silently behind him, like a faithful wingman.

Mercanary appreciates that command of a style brings a certain timbre and that one can explode meaning.

Upon reaching this zenith, Harry's jaw drops at the sight of this studio full of nudes. Life-sized photographs of men and women of all shapes, colours, and sizes are scattered and layered in stacks along the walls, resting against tables and shelves, filling the entire field of view and obscuring what must be an amazing view of scenic downtown St. John's. The studio space is a collage of fleshy forms, and Rei stands in the centre of it all, reflecting.

Harry's awestruck.

Mercanary agrees.

Rei is sharply attired in a black pantsuit with a white blouse. Two messy buns in her hair are twisted in place with red pens. She's making notes on a clipboard when she sees Harry perched at the top of the spiral staircase.

"Don't be shy," she says. "I know you."

"You do," Harry responds with a grin. "There's

a lot to take in here."

"I know." Rei turns to face Harry, laying down the clipboard. "It can be hard for some."

"I don't mind hard. I just didn't expect this."

"No? What were you expecting?"

"Well, I dunno. I – "

"This?" She clutches Harry's jacket in her hands, pulling him to her, and she kisses him like she's hungry for it.

Harry can't believe his good fortune, and he goes with it.

What is this, a porno?

No, but it may come close.

With moist lips and darting tongues, their hands fish for buttons and flies. Everything comes off in a flurry and in no particular order.

The two don't speak. They communicate in grunts and getures, gasps and grasps.

Mercanary leans against the stair's rail, tossing some popcorn into the air and catching each piece with his beak, pecking wildly into the air after each kernel.

Mercanary appreciates the unstirred.

The embraced pair shuffle across the studio to Rei's desk. She throws her notes to the floor and hops her bare ass onto the cold oak. She shivers at the touch of the wood. Harry's thrilled.

About fifteen minutes later, Harry's pulling his jeans back on, one leg at a time, when he introduces himself.

"So, yeah, I'm Harry."

"I know, Harry," Rei replies. She laughs and adds, "We met at your party, dude. Fuck! You think I'd just fuck the fish-n-chips guy all random like that?"

"What? No."

"What the fuck? Shit, Harry. What kind of girl do you think I am?"

"I just remember bumping into you when you left in the morning." Harry remembers learning her name at the top of the stairs that night, too, but he doesn't admit that part.

"Harry, we drank absinthe. I remember Scarlett introducing us. Then, I made you a drink, and you loved the flaming sugar cube bit, but then you disappeared into the night."

"Yeah, that sounds about right."

Who knows?

"I'm fucking with you, Harry. I'm Rei."

Harry smiles and laughs it off. He appears relieved.

Mercanary raises an eyebrow and squints to see Rei more clearly. He's less impressed.

Rei buttons up her slacks. "This was exactly what I ordered. This was nice."

"I'd rate that as better than nice, but I'll take what I can get."

Rei giggles, and she adds, "That wasn't my professional critique of your performance, you know."

"It wasn't?"

"No. I'm saving that review for *The Overpass*."

"Fuck off!"

"You were marvellous, Harry." She exaggerates each syllable but it still coddles his ego, and then she adds, "I'm just foolin'."

Mercanary raises an eyebrow and looks at you.

You shrug.

"Work's going to go well now this afternoon."

"Yes, I'm sure it will," Harry agrees.

Mercanary mimics looking at a watch that he isn't wearing on his wing, and then Harry remembers his other deliveries.

"Shit! I've got to run!" Harry pulls on his sneakers and scrambles for the stairs.

"I left you a nice tip through the app!" Rei yells

out to him across the studio.

"Thanks!" Harry's certainly not unhappy, even though he knows that tip will be shared with Spence and Roz.

He snatches up the three carriers near the exit, and, with Mercanary at his side, they run from the gallery to Specific Place.

Harry's breathing threatens to burst his lungs, but he pushes onward, trying to make up time. He takes the elevator to the top and resumes his routine for the regulars. They are understanding. A twenty-minute delay is reasonable on occassion.

He's reached the ground floor again when he notices he still hasn't delivered the special order for the law firm. His stomach lurches. He takes the elevator back to the top floor, and he finds Sullivan, Fielding, and Bull in suite 1090-1110. He hits the door's buzzer, and the receptionist lets him inside.

"Hey, sorry about the delay," Harry offers an apology.

"You're forty five minutes late," says the receptionist. He is not pleased because he's been the one delivering the message to his employers that the catering hasn't arrived yet. He's had to deliver a variation of that message seven times already.

Mercanary appreciates a good line or two.

"Yeah, about that, I – "

"We aren't paying for this. You'll have to issue a refund."

"What? But, there must be 300 bucks of fish here?"

"Yeah, cold fish, and we won't be paying for it." The receptionist reiterates this flatly as he sorts through the orders, matching each with his list for the hungry bosses and clients.

Harry's at a loss.

"Fine. You'll have to deal with Roz. I can't issue that sort of refund."

"We'll be speaking to her, certainly."

Mercanary looks at Harry with a glint of hope in his eye, but Harry just shakes his head, picks up the empty carriers, and returns to the elevator.

His thoughts are of Rei as he walks back to Wiggly's. Forget about the deliveries. He figures he's done, but he remembers Bob told him something about another gig, so he's not really concerned.

Mercanary appreciates normal wasn't normal to begin with anyway.

The second he's back at Wiggly's, Roz lets him know he's done.

He agrees.

Spence listens in from beside the cutting table.

Roz says he'll have to pay for that catering order himself.

Harry accepts that.

She says he won't be sharing the day's tips.

He's fine with that, too.

She says he's fired.

He says he quits.

Spence snorts.

Mercanary does the dance of joy as Harry gathers his belongings from the back, and then they leave Wiggly's behind for good.

Mercanary appreciates too much as a relative concept.

That afternoon, Harry writes a steamy review of *Another Dory Story* on his phone while sipping coffee in his car. It doesn't take him long to finish it, so he drafts some ideas for a short screenplay to pass the time. He's parked at Signal Hill, looking out to the distant horizon along the ocean's edge.

That evening, Harry tells his roommates he quit working for Wiggly's. He doesn't give them the details but says he has another gig lined up already through Bob.

Later that evening, Harry and Mercanary go to see Bob about a job.

Hermeneutical Algebra

Life is art is philosophy is art is life,

Not
Life is philosophy is art is philosophy is life,

Not
Philosophy is art is life is art is philosophy,

Not even
Art is life is philosophy is life is art,

Nor
Philosophy is life is art is life is philosophy,

Just
Life is art is philosophy is art is life.

Suspended

nlwx
yyt
no filter
no fx
freezing rain
icedrop
twirling
twirling
twirling towards freedom
unable to get there
suspended in air
i feel ya

In Space

Captain Don Key and the Mercanary™ in
"Friday Night's Alright for Fighting"

Welcome back, peerless viewers, to another exciting instalment of *Captain Don Key and the Mercanary*™, the daring space adventure series that knows no bounds and heeds no warnings!

When last we saw our impulsive heroes, they had discovered Rock-It Shark's twisted plot to stone the universe. Having accidentally discovered an obsure audio frequency that petrifies listeners, Rock-It Shark had promptly recorded a classic-rock-styled power ballad with his solo project, in which he plays every instrument and sings all the harmonies. It was a nightmarish scene, but the song is undeniably attractive to its target demographic: spacers of the desperate sort. Our heroes discovered this offensive scheme thanks to the ever-precious resourcefulness of the pilot of the *Exit Prize*, Ruth "Gem" Morgemsdottir, who had overheard Rock-It Shark bragging about it at the Intergalactic Urban Sound Exchange while she was in search of a new needle for the starship's phonograph. Knowing of the hefty illicit bounty placed on subduing Rock-It Shark alive, Gem suggested to Captain Don Key and Mercanary that they track the hideous creature to his lair with the *Exit Prize*. After a perplexing conversation with Mercanary, Key stole credit for the idea, and they were on their way.

We return to our heroes on spacedate 978-1-927-996-08-9, a Friday. In this episode, we find the *Exit Prize* parked outside the garage of a tiny warehouse on a crumbling rock in the darkness of space – the remnants of a long-dead planetoid – known only now as Albertasteroid. Inside, we find an electrified sound board and smoking amplifiers along with our heroes celebrating their swift triumph over Rock-It Shark, who is bound and muzzled, laid out on the ground, snout in a grease puddle, back under Key's boot, and with a large cork crammed up the rocket that is his lower torso.

Mercanary wipes the dust of the scuffle from his feathered wings, wiping his fishy tail across a welcome mat near the door. His beak beams with a self-satisfied smile, and Key looks just as pleased with himself.

Forgetting the sonic-nullifying earguards they are both wearing, Key boasts, "That was easy money! Who would've thought we could thwart Rock-It Shark's villainous scheme with mere earmuffs?"

"CHIRP! CHIRP!" Mercanary squawks in reply, seeing Key mouthing something inaudible.

"What!?" Key shouts. "I can't hear you! Mercanary, why can't I hear you?"

"COO! COO!"

"What?"

"COO!"

"You can't hear me because you're still wearing those blasted earmuffs, Mercanary! Take those off!" Key commands, pantomiming the removal of earmuffs by removing his own.

Mercanary removes his, too, and quips, "Chirp."

"Yes, I know! We do, indeed, deserve to celebrate," Key responds just as a breeze from the open garage door allows his half-cape to billow out behind him, exposing his hairless, hyper-muscular chest, making his tassles dance slightly. Although he turned pirate the day he met the mercanary and claimed the Transgalactic Space Fleet patrol-ship as his own and christened it the *Exit Prize*, he still refuses to dress in anything other than the fleet's ceremonial uniform: a silver half-cape, clasped around the neck; no shirt or jacket of any sort; a pair of tassled pasties cover the nipples, the gold signifying the rank of captain; silver pantaloons to match the half-cape; a white leather utility belt, holstering a blaster and ludicrous gadgets; and a pair of white leather boots equipped with vicious metal spurs that clink with each step. The get-up marks some sort of dignity in Key's mind, but it never hurts to be clad in the guise of the TSF, as its influence can be leveraged on occasion.

Static crackles through their communicators, and a muffled voice calls out, "Are you boys okay in there?" It's Gem calling from the cockpit of the *Exit Prize*. Our heroes turn to peer out the garage door at the ship. She waves from the pilot's seat, feet casually resting on the dash.

"Yes," replies Key. "He's down, the device is destroyed, and we're in the mood to celebrate!"

"COO! COO!" Mercanary confirms, waving his wings about wildly.

"Great," Gem adds. "We'll just collect the bounty on Rock-It Shark – wait. He is alive, right?"

"Of course he is," Key assures her. "But the payday can wait. We're going to get drunk first!"

"CHIRP!"

"What? Why can't we collect the bounty first?" Gem inquires with some frustation.

"There are still some credits in our coffer," Key asserts. "We'll blow that tonight, and then refill it tomorrow when we cash in Rock-It Shark."

"CHIRP! CHIRP!"

"Mercanary agrees," Key continues. "This is the smart move. And, it will be good for morale! Set course for the nearest drinking district that will welcome us!"

"Sure," Gem relents. "The nearest 'welcoming' drinking district is back home, and that's not even close."

"Ugh," Key groans. "So be it! Set course for Town, Newfoundmoon and Labraplanet! Park in the Anchor Zone; we're not heading to the Outports tonight."

"You're the captain," Gem replies as she enters the coordinates and primes the engine.

Captain Don Key and Mercanary board the starship, leave the captive Rock-It Shark on a couch in the ship's lounge, and enter the cockpit.

"Buckle up, losers!" Gem cries as she grips the throttle. "Take-off might get a bit rough."

The *Exit Prize*'s hyperlight nacelles sputter and then blaze with a fierce yellow energy, and the ship launches forward, abruptly turning upwards and into the vast emptiness of space. With the cheapest engine in the solar system, the flight home is lengthy.

As they hurtle across the galaxies, the three

heroes carry on with their usual inane banter.

"... and when I met Mercanary down by the breakwater, this beast-thing was armed to the beak with antique machine guns," Key remembered. He loved telling this story, and he often embellished it. "He was born out of nothing, as far as I could tell, in a fantastic cacophony of gunfire! I was entirely enthralled, so I introduced myself, we hit it off, and – after many a misadventure – here we are!"

"CHIRP! CHIRP!" Mercanary bleats with vigour.

"Yes, yes," Key accepts Mercanary's correction of the details. "I know you're a mystical being or a mythical bean or whatever. Of course you are! Look at you! Anyway, after we sold those antiques, we had enough money to refuel the *Exit Prize*, and that's how we financed our first expedition."

"Right. It all makes sense now, after hearing this again for the thousandth time," Gem listlessly concedes, as she curls up in the pilot's seat, having little to do now that the ship was on-course besides humouring these two. She rocks the chair so that her ponytail falls over the back. She pulls her mechanic's cap down a little over her eyes and continues, "Sometimes I don't know how you two survived before bringing me along."

"It wasn't long until we found you, Gem," Key replies, unwittingly acknowledging their absurd luck.

"COO!" Mercanary interjects.

"Yes, we were rather fortunate that that was the case, Mercanary," Key agrees.

Later, while the *Exit Prize* enters the Milkiest Way, the cluster of galaxies our impulsive heroes call home, Key and Mercanary retire to the lounge to check the durability of Rock-It Shark's electro-manacles.

"Now, struggle!" Key commands as he switches on the electro-manacles' shock-and-stun feature.

Z-Z-Z-ZAP!

"MMMMMPH!" Rock-It Shark screams despite his muzzle, twisting and convulsing under the pulsing shocks.

"Coo," Mercanary observes.

"No. This will suffice," Key decides. "This villain won't escape his bonds. They're secured sturdily enough around his fins, and the shock hasn't loosened that cork, either. This is fine."

"Chirp-chirp," Mercanary adds.

"No, Mercanary. Where can he even go? We're in space. There's nothing to be concerned about. He's secure enough here."

The *Exit Prize* glides past Labraplanet on its preset course to Newfoundmoon. Other ships crowd the space orbiting the planet and the moon. Both of these celestial bodies have seen better

191

days, but now they are primarily frequented by miners, pirates, wreckers, garbage tycoons, and those who simply cannot afford an escape. Mining ships export what is left of the resources, and garbage barges import intergalactic waste to fill the void. The result is a handful of spaceports, only one of which could be called bustling, and that is Town.

Gem manually docks the starship in the Anchor Zone of Town. The loading door opens to a haze of noxious smog that the locals only call fog. It's a sort of coping mechanism to deny the amount of sketch in the air. Workers of every species process cargo and supplies – some are tentacled octopeds, some are upright crustaceans, some have horns, and some have mouth mandibles. None of this is unusual here, even if humans were the founding species many millenia ago.

The three heroes disembark.

"So long, Rock-It Shark," Key yells over his shoulder. "We'll cash you in tomorrow. Sit tight!"

"COO! COO!" Mercanary threatens.

"Yeah, or else," Key adds, snatching the last word.

The sky over Newfoundmoon is three shades of grey. It is still Friday. It is nighttime, too, but our viewers would be forgiven for thinking it was daylight. The light from an ever-precarious greenhouse never permits the skies to darken fully, only allowing these shifting shades of grey. Never you mind that our special effects budget has been slashed three times this year. Maybe one of our faithful viewers would like to invest in our esteemed production. Maybe that is you! Anyway, Labraplanet's silhouette can be discerned through the overcast only by those who first know where to look in the night sky.

Tonight, the fog is thick and wet. Our heroes walk along the streets of Town, passing along buildings that were once – surely – as colourful as a handful of jelly beans. The fog, however, has covered everything with layers of grime. Things look slimy.

"I mean, how do you even pull a trigger with those wings of yours?" Key asks Mercanary in all honesty as they walk from the Anchor Zone towards Jarge Street.

"COO!"

"Yes, I know that, but ..."

"COO! COO!"

"Right. I know that, too, but ..." Key pauses as he is drowned out by the rumbling of a passing garbage convoy.

"Give him a break, Don," Gem interrupts. "It's not like he ever hassles you about your half-cape."

"CHIRP!"

"M-my uniform is a symbol of my authority," Key stammers, not hurt but frustrated that he must reiterate its importance.

"COO!"

"Hahahaha! Even Mercanary knows no one looks at it like that, Don," Gem chides.

"I'll overlook your jest, pilot," Key permits, "but only because we have reached our destination. Behold!" Key gestures to the rusty gate that marks the entrance to Jarge Street, a short lane of bars upon bars and drunks upon drunks. The three enter a bar called the Rocket House, a club known to all sorts of spacers and a not-too-shabby establishment for Jarge Street.

About four hours or so later, Key comes hurtling out the door of another bar, Kara's Karaoke's Okay, Okay, a somewhat shabbier karaoke bar on the other end of Jarge Street.

"I cannot believe you do not have 9/10 Bros.," Key exclaims as he is thrown through the door and out onto the street by the bouncer, a hulking urban champion sort of bloke with a tattered t-shirt and bright blue hair. Mercanary and Gem squeeze through the door together, pushing past the urban champion, and lifting their captain from the muddy concrete. Key now wears an eyepatch. He curses back at the bouncer, "I'll be damned if I can't have a go at singing some 9/10 Bros. Don't make me come back there! I shall smite you with my power glove!"

"CHIRP! CHIRP!" Mercanary scowls at the bouncer, gritting his beak.

"And the mercanary shall hex you, you bulky brute!" Key regains his footing just before tripping over the curbside. The bouncer turns away, unamused.

Gem catches Key before he can collapse, and she suggests, "Let's get you some fries, dressing, and gravy, Don. You likes fries, dressing, and gravy. You knows you do. C'mon we goes, and I'll get a taco."

As the three stumble towards a vendor selling chips, Key's spurs clink sadly along the cobblestones. He looks around at the other patrons of Jarge Street. Myriad faces on bodies all blur before his gaze. People are enjoying themselves, but there are a few snorts of disgust heard nearby, as if someone was just insulted.

Gem orders two lots of chips for Key and Mercanary.

"Here," she says, and she hands them the food. "Soak up some of the booze in your bellies before we get back to the ship. I'll be back once I score a taco from YOLO. Don't make an ass of yourself while I'm gone." That last remark she aims more at Key than Mercanary.

A few minutes pass in silence as Key and Mercanary sit on a canopied deck eating their chips, casually scanning the crowd. Key looks up and down the street. Most people are on the move, but some loiter. Club-goers mill about outside a club, vaping from a shared hookah carried in a satchel. They are chatting and laughing, having a good time. A pair of lovers embrace in an alley, stealing a semi-private moment for themselves, no fewer than twelve tentacles writhing in plain sight, all the same. A group of humanoid jellyfish float along down the road carrying guitar cases and a keyboard, chatting pleasantly amongst themselves. One of them has an unusual face for a jellyfish, however. It stands out to Key. The ghostly visage looks kind of like a troll-cat.

Key does a double take.

It looks exactly like a troll-cat! In fact, it is the very face of the one and only Troll-Cat, Key and Mercanary's archnemesis!

Squinting, Key goes for the triple take, but the face has disappeared. The jellyfish walk down the street, bickering amongst themselves now.

With some disbelief, Key shakes his head briskly, hoping to shake the image of Troll-Cat as well.

Then, another haunting image catches his eye.

The man with the vape-satchel now has the face of Troll-Cat!

Key blinks rapidly and rubs his eyes, but the image is gone, like wisps of vapours. The vapers are only talking with their friend, but they are no longer laughing.

"You know, Mercanary," Key states firmly, "I swear I must be proper shagged up tonight. I keep seeing Troll-Cat, our archnemesis, everywhere I look. And, I do mean everywhere! Like, it is as if his face is transposed onto every drunk on Jarge Street! Seriously. This can't be right."

"Coo?" Mercanary asks.

"Yes," Key replies. "I must be quite inebriated."

"Chirp, chirp," Mercanary offers in consolation.

Then a shriek bellows forth from the tentacled lovers in the alleyway. "Quit sucking so hard! Get your tentacles off me!"

Mercanary and Key both turn toward the source of the commotion and each of them spots the ethereal face of Troll-Cat hovering about the lecherous perpetrator. It seems to leave the tentacled humanoid, it floats about in the air only briefly, and then it vanishes into the thick, grimy fog. Nevertheless, they both saw this happen.

"Troll-Cat has somehow possessed that lady and is abusing that poor octo-lad," Key shouts as he attempts to make sense of the situation.

"Coo, coo. Co–" Mercanary cautions, but it is too late.

"No," Key rejects such a cautionary and logical explanation, and he bounds forth to save the day.

The tentacled woman seems confused, the tentacled man is flailing a flurry of limbs to keep her at bay, and Key charges in with his fist raised behind him, yelling "Unhand that lad! RRRRAAARRRRGH!"

There is a blind swing and a heavy thud, and when Key opens his one good eye, the tentacled man is on the ground, since the tentacled woman dodged his punch.

"What do you think you're doing!?" The tentacled woman demands an answer for this swift and brutal transgression.

"Uhhh," Key fails at an articulate response.

"I black out for a second, and Archie turns against me, and then you come running over here and nailed my Archie!" The octo-lady is confused but rightly irate.

"CHIRP!" Mercanary offers as an explanation.

"What?" The lady asks impatiently. "What are you even saying?"

"CHIRP! CHIRP!"

"I can't make any sense of that," she replies as the lad on the ground regains his senses, standing up on his four tentacles, his other tentacles clutching around his throbbing cheek. "You expect me to believe that some space ghost, who happens to be your arch-nemesis, has been possessing people on Jarge Street just to sow gloom? That's unreal!"

Luckily, Gem notices the commotion and rushes over to diffuse the situation. Mercanary shields Key with his wing, just as the octo-lady shields Archie from his assailants.

"Tentacled sir," Gem calls out as she approaches. "Good tentacled sir! I'm really sorry about my boss here. He's a real ass."

"Cherleen," the lad asks his partner, "what just happened? You suddenly weren't yourself, getting all sucky and feely, and you wouldn't quit it. I told you to quit it. That wasn't like you at all. And then, it was like I could see some other face, like it was on top of your own. It was gruesome, with the droopiest eyes I have ever seen!" He shudders, but accepts Cherleen's comforting embrace. "And then! This cop slugs me in the face!"

"Oh, no, no, no, no, no," Gem says quickly. "He's not a cop. I mean, he says he used to be a cop, but I really can't say for sure. I know he's not a cop now. He's definitely not a cop now."

Cherleen and Archie shake their heads and

slither off into the night, happy to go anywhere but on Jarge Street with these lunatics.

"Chirp, chirp," Mercanary explains to Gem.

"I see," Gem replies. "So, you're both convinced that Troll-Cat has somehow developed the means to possess people at-will from an undetermined distance. I mean, you both claim to have witnessed the ghostly face of Troll-Cat, just floating around, bothering people, and sowing gloom. Okay. Let's accept that as given and go from there. You walk off the drunkeness, and I'll meet you back at the ship."

They do just that. Mercanary helps Key along, and they all leave the scene before any real cops can arrive. Gem goes straight to work.

"How will we ever find Troll-Cat, Mercanary?" Key asks with little hope.

"Coo," replies Mercanary.

"I mean, he wasn't even there in bodily form, right? So often we best our nemesis, but he could be anywhere," Key despairs.

Once Key and Mercanary return to the ship, Gem greets them with excitement. "It's all set! Not only do I have a plan, but I made a short animated film. It explains everything. Someone has to watch out for you two goofs. This is the unrated cut."

"CHIRP!" cries Mercanary as he plops Key

down beside Rock-It Shark on the couch.

"Thanks, Merc," she says, then she dims the lights in the lounge and flips a switch on the projector.

The animated sequence begins with fanfare and an impressive logo. The film highlights, with impeccable comedic effect, the entire span of their night – beginning with their landing in the Anchor Zone strolling through Town to Jarge Street and doing shots at the Rocket House, it also portrays: Mercanary's striptease at Turkey Moe's; Gem's enthusiastic moshing to the incomparable Tubasonics at Club Zero; Key's fight with a watermelonoid at Treble's Base, in which he ends up half-blind; the trio's frightful attempt to croon along with the infamous Catalina Wreckers at the Starship Inn; their getting thrown out of Kara's Karaoke's Okay, Okay; and Gem's re-imagining of the encounter with the apparition of Troll-Cat, which takes great liberties in recreating the scene that Mercanary had described to her.

"Oh! Here's where I detail my plan," Gem announces with pride.

The film shows an animated Gem flicking through the starship's rolodex until she finds the last known address of Troll-Cat.

"He's listed in our bloody rolodex," exclaims Captain Don Key with apparent disbelief.

"Yeah," Gem replies coolly. "This isn't your first rodeo. Once you hired me, I started keeping tabs on your recurring antagonists. He's been working out of a loft in a small warehouse on Fogtown Alley for years now. You guys should know this. We've been there before, more than once, and he never moves out."

"Set a course for Fogtown Alley," Key commands.

"But, there's more to my plan," Gem insists.

"COO! COO!"

"Whatever," Key persists. "Fly us there! Immediately! Before I grow more sober. Park on his roof if you have to."

"You're the boss, Captain," and Gem switches the projector off and sits behind the starship's controls.

The *Exit Prize* quickly launches from the spacedock, only to fly a kilometer down the road to pitch on the roof of a warehouse situated along Fogtown Alley. The loading door opens, and our three heroes step out onto the debris-covered rooftop, the ship's exhaust contributing to the fog.

"Mercanary and I shall see to Troll-Cat. Gem, you stay here and guard the *Exit Prize*."

"Yeah. I'll do just that, Don."

Mercanary bravely leads the way through the

202

roof's entrance while Key stands safely behind the beast-thing. Gem stands near the cargo door, puffing her vape, until the other two disappear inside. She takes another long haul, breathes vapour into the air, it blends in with the fog, and then she strolls across the rooftop.

The stairway inside the warehouse is dark, but light flickers on the first floor down from Key and Mercanary.

"This must be Troll-Cat's lair," Key proclaims. Mercanary nods in agreement, and then Key kicks down the door, bursting into a laboratory that is in shambles. Seated behind a mess of cables, coils, and doo-dads is their loathsome enemy Troll-Cat, just as Gem had predicted.

"A-HA!" Key shouts as he rushes into the lab. "Troll-Cat, the jig is up! You shall cause no more trouble with your sick schemes and foul machines!"

"WhaaaAAAaaaaaAAAAt-t-t-t-t?" Troll-Cat croaks. "Mercanary? And, Key? How did you two dolts find me?"

"Forget about that," Key dismisses his question. "How are you thrusting your psyche upon innocent drunks? What are you up to, Troll-Cat?"

"CHIRP! CHIRP! COO!"

"That's right, Mercanary," Troll-Cat admits, "I will obliterate the self-esteem of everyone in the

203

solar system – one-by-one if I have to – but you haven't figured out all of it just yet. You see, earlier, I was simply testing my latest invention, the psychic possession projector, when you caught a glimpse of my projected psyche on Jarge Street. I saw you there, too, long before you noticed me. What you fail to realize is: I have completed my tests. Now, I possess a fully functioning psychic possession projector! MUAH-HAHAHAHA! Patents are pending."

Just as he finishes his speech, Troll-Cat dons a bulky helmet with protruding electrodes and cables that connect to other surrounding machinery. Placing this helm on his head, great sparks of electricty shoot forth yet nothing explodes. Then, before Key and Mercanary can take any action, the ethereal form of Troll-Cat separates from his bodily form, and it glides across the room towards Mercanary, cramming itself down his beak and into his head.

"NOOOOO!" Key shouts, fumbling for his blaster, too late to save his friend from possession.

"YESSSS," Mercanary replies, a ghostly image of Troll-Cat fading in and out around Mercanary's head.

"This can't be so!"

"But, it is so," Troll-Cat says to Key through Mercanary's own beak. "You wouldn't harm a feather on your dearest friend, would you?"

The possessed Mercanary takes flight for a moment, then swoops at Key, who tries to duck while firing his blaster – hitting his dear friend squarely in the breast, but the mythical merbird is undeterred – and Mercanary plucks him up by the half-cape, and drops him unceremoniously into a pile of rubbish.

Disoriented and still a bit drunk, Key doesn't know what to do here. How can he fight his treasured friend? He hasn't worked it out just yet, and Mercanary is already on him again, lifting him from the trash and tossing him against a support beam, where he secures Key with chains and an old lock.

"This can't be going as you planned," Troll-Cat says to Key through Mercanary. Meanwhile, Troll-Cat's body remains with his gear, wearing the electrified psychic possession projector helm.

Key grimaces. He struggles against the chains. He is stuck and distraught.

The lights flicker, and then they go out.

Next, there is a fearsome cawing, followed by rustling feathers, then a swoosh cuts through the air. There is a loud commotion, including a series of knocks, bumps, and thuds. After the final crack, the only sound is a gurgling groan.

When the lights come back on, Mercanary is standing over Troll-Cat's unconscious form on the floor, the psychic possession projector – the helmet and the rest of the equipment – is broken to bits and scattered across the floor with the other garbage.

"You did it, Mercanary," Key shrieks with joy from his bonds.

Mercanary nods, flattening his dishevelled feathers to look more respectable.

Gem coolly saunters into the disrupted evil laboratory.

"Mercanary, you did it," she says with calm sincerity. "I knew you'd follow through once I had disabled the back-up generators and cut the power."

"That was you, Gem?" Key asks with some astonishment.

"Don, I told you I had a plan."

"She totally did," Mercanary confirms. "Good call, Gem. Thanks for saving the day! You're a real gem."

Gem and Key turn abruptly to their friend, jaws dropped and awestruck.

Key exclaims, "You can speak!"

"Well, yeah," Mercanary responds concisely. "Key! Dude! You shot me!"

What was that?

Will the friendship of Captain Don Key and Mercanary survive such a reckless attack?

Will Gem have the patience to put up with their relentless antics?

Will our impulsive heroes find more thrilling misadventures on Newfoundmoon?

Will there be any meaningful consequences?

Tune in next time, dearest viewers, to find out if you'll have satisfactory answers to any of your questions! If the show isn't cancelled before then, then maybe you can see for yourself in "The Mercanary Speaks" or "What Ever Happened to Rock-It Shark?"

Coded

"Just like old times, eh, friend?" Bob asks from shotgun.

Mercanary appreciates Madonna's epic-level glove game since at least '94.

"Bob, you know I'm trying to steer clear of this shit, right?"

It's late. It's dark and the roads are wet, but these two're already on the highway, en route. Mercanary's riding in the back seat, scoping out the moonlit countryside as they speed along the asphalt.

"Just this last run, Harry," Bob assures him, but after a moment's pause he adds, "You're getting paid well for this. It's just driving. All you're doing is driving, and I know you're in a pinch now, so I won't hold you to this being the last one. I'll forgive you that."

"I'm not looking for forgiveness. I just want to

work. Geezus, can't I make a buck legally?"

"All. You. Are. Doing. Is. DRIVING." Bob resents Harry's attitude about this sort of work – this is a Barthes family tradition, after all – but they're in this together again, for now.

"Right."

"You drive me to the dock, and we'll go for a little ride. It'll be quick. Drive me back home in the morning, and you're free until next time."

"I'm just trying to let you know, man. I get too paranoid doing this shit. It wore me out years ago. I can't be at it, b'y."

"Yeah." Bob's not buying it.

"I got you this time. I know Andre's gone to Alberta for work, but this is the only time I'm filling in."

"So you say."

"So I do."

"Well, this is romantic," Mercanary says, but, with the resulting lull in the conversation, he lies down across the back seat for a nap.

Mercanary appreciates Yoshimi's efforts throughout all of this.

Harry grips the wheel and squints to see the lines on the highway. He turns off the Trans Canada onto the Burin Highway. Bob picks through a steel case of compact discs, pulling the first Gorillaz album from its sleeve and sliding it into the player in the dash.

"You remember this track?" Bob asks.

"Dude, I still listen to this all the time!"

"S'right, son! 'Sunshine in a bag!'"

"Fuckin' right."

"That's what it's all about."

"Not all of it."

"All of it, and you know – "

A small shadow is suddenly on the road.

Harry slams his foot onto the brake.

The wheels screech.

Mercanary jerks himself erect.

A black cat makes eye contact with Harry, gazing past the car's headlights, its eyes flashing yellow.

Harry swerves and the car hydroplanes.

"AHHHHHHH!" Harry, Bob, and Mercanary yell in chorus as the car spins thrice around before coming to a stop.

"What the fuck was that for, Harry?"

Harry doesn't reply. He opens his door to size up the scene, standing with one foot still inside the vehicle.

> Mercanary appreciates a good Garfield-sans-Garfield.

No other cars are in sight.

He didn't hear a thump.

He doesn't see any remains in front of the vehicle, so he scans the sidelines, finding nothing.

"Harry?"

Harry steps out of the car and peeps under it.

There it is, entirely unconcerned just inches from the front bumper.

"Harry! What the fuck, man? Get back in the car! You'll be satched! It's probably just a rabbit or a fox, anyway."

The cat is drenched with rain. It looks more feral than it is, and it saunters off to the gas station's dumpsters nearby.

Harry's a little shaken, but he plops back into the driver's seat with a pop.

With a pop?

Yes, with a pop, and the pop is followed by a deep, steady hiss.

Bob's jaw drops. He and Harry share a knowing look, recognizing the sounds for what they signify.

Mercanary looks back and forth between the

211

two, not quite understanding the misery of changing a flat tire in the rain on a cold, dark highway.

> Mercanary appreciates clear messaging on merch while still valuing masks.

This scene is about what you'd expect.

Bob's not pleased, but he helps Harry push the car to the side of the road before letting Harry take it from there. Mercanary watches with glee, since he's never been bothered by rain.

Meanwhile, Bob's supervising as Harry gets the spare, jacks the car, removes the flat, heaves it in the trunk, attaches the spare, lowers the car, and stores the gear in the back.

Other than the sound of the fully cranked heater, the remainder of the drive to Fortune is quiet.

They don't bother to get a room. They're here on business, and Bob has to make up for lost time. They're already running late.

The three collect Bob's boat, *The Happiest Adventure*, from a Barthes' warehouse. The family handles the business's imports and exports through Fortune. This is how (and why) they have the yacht.

It's not that odd.

> Mercanary appreciates Weird Al's nuanced understanding of camouflage.

It's already past 2 a.m. by the time they get the keel wet and set sail into the night.

The rain pelts the cabin's windshield as Bob guides the wheel. Harry holds the rail, knowing he's never really gotten his sea legs sorted out. Mercanary clutches at the yacht's bow and, despite the torrential downpour, loudly boasts this parody, "'I'M THE KING OF THE WORLD!'"

Mercanary appreciates that the artist is the voice of each character created.

The lights along Newfoundland's coast dim in the distance as they sail to the rendezvous.

Somewhere in the sea between Fortune and France, another ship flashes a signal. The centre of its three foglights blinks – dash, dot, dash, dot – then it pauses, and then it repeats. Harry watches as Bob flips a light switch of his own – dash, dot, dot. The other ship's light ceases blinking.

"This is new," Harry says.

"We've had to upgrade precautions after that scare with da b'ys from Marystown."

"Yeah?"

"It's a long story," Bob admits. "Morse Code, oui? He says C, I reply D, and then we meet."

"Sounds like everything's ship shape," Mercanary chimes, popping his head up from behind the cabin's minifridge.

213

Harry laughs. "What're the letters for?"

"Cheval and dick."

Harry laughs again. "What?"

"Another long story. Next time."

"Not a chance."

The two smirk.

"I'm going to need you to help with this."

"What happened to just driving, eh?"

"Driving and lifting, then. I'm paying, yeah? C'mon, don't give me a hard time here. He'll be pissed we're so late, and I don't like it when he's pissy."

"Alright," Harry relents. "No worries. What needs doin'?"

"Just heave a line across when I come up alongside her. Maurice will drop his plank."

"Eh, b'y."

Mercanary appreciates the real heroes more than the myths.

Harry dons his oilskins before going out onto the deck. The sea isn't rough, not really, but Harry wouldn't know that. With his lack of experience, the bobbing waves could be a predecessor to the perfect storm. They aren't, but he'd never know it. It makes him nervous, but he does his job, tossing

214

the line to a crewman aboard *Le Mythe*, a fishing vessel, old and barnacled but with an extra large hold. The two ships come together in the night. A boarding plank is returned, and Harry secures his end.

Bob comes on deck and ties another line tossed from *Le Mythe*. The seamen are silent. Harry thinks they look tired and impatient, probably because of the delay. It's not like Bob's going to break radio silence just because he's behind.

"Alright," Bob beckons to Harry, "Give da b'ys a hand loading the cargo, will ya?"

"Shit. You weren't kidding about the lifting."

"Not for a second."

"I'll help," Mercanary offers, swooping between the two, relishing the salty rainfall.

"I need to speak with Maurice about his horse. I'll come once we've finished. You just help da b'ys here. They won't bite. This won't be long."

"Good enough," Harry accepts.

"He'll be pissy."

"Is this going to be trouble?"

"No. It means it should go quickly. Just store everything in the master bedroom's floor. You know the hold I mean."

"Yeah, I remember. S'all good. Do your thing."

Mercanary appreciates complex origin stories.

Harry assists the other crewmen to move cooler after cooler from one hold to the other. The crates vary in weight but not size. Harry grunts as he carries the heavier ones, and then he slows his pace. The others show no sign of easing up, so Mercanary sings this shanty to improve morale: "These shadowy men / Have a shadowy racket. / Their bounty's the booty. / Shown booty, they pack it!"

Harry laughs.

You laugh.

Everybody laughs.

Mercanary appreciates that local support means a lot and so do you.

The work of packing booty takes less than an hour, but Bob's still occupied with Maurice.

The French crew return to *Le Mythe*, and Harry waits alone with Mercanary on the deck of *The Happiest Adventure*.

Mercanary appreciates some brilliant people have written farce. Mercanary also appreciates Aesop as much as Plato as much as Lovecraft as much as Wallace as much as Darwin as much as Goldman as much as Atwood.

The plank still bridges the gap as the ships bob up and down, nearly synchronous.

216

Harry looks to Mercanary as if enough time has passed already, and Mercanary nods.

"Fuck it," Harry says. "I'm going to see what's up."

"Dude. Enough is enough. It's time we get this ship back on the road!"

Harry boards *Le Mythe*. The crew have gone below. Mercanary floats in the air over Harry's shoulders as he opens the door to the bridge.

"Harry!" Bob shrieks.

"Merde," Maurice adds over Bob's shoulder.

"What the fuck, man!?!" Bob's furious. He jerks his pants from his ankles to his waist.

"OHHHHHH!"

"What the actual fuck! I said I'd be back when we were finished here."

"I didn't expect – "

"You didn't listen!"

"Is this going to be trouble?" Maurice asks Bob with ice in his timbre. He turns away, adjusts his manhood, and zips up his fly.

"Fuck no," Bob answers.

"Fuck no!" Harry takes a step back from the doorway.

"Not a fuckin' chance!" Mercanary dives into

the sea without making a ripple.

> Mercanary appreciates one can't practice magic without having first studied the art.

Bob implores, "Maurice, listen – "

"Next time."

"Sure. Okay. It's like that. Okay."

"Bob – "

"Shut. The. Fuck up, Harry!"

"Done."

At that, Bob shoots Harry a look to kill.

Harry raises his hands and walks away. He doesn't hear the remainder of what Bob and Maurice have to say to one another. He'll never learn those details.

Bob unties *The Happiest Adventure* from *Le Mythe*. He doesn't let Harry help. He shoos him to the wheelhouse.

Mercanary gives the two friends some space, dive-bombing a school of herring for a quick snack.

Wind and rain batter at the windows as Bob lays out the terms to Harry.

First, he says, "Marg knows, so don't tell her anything about it."

"Gotcha," Harry agrees. "Of course."

218

"Be quiet."

Harry almost responds, but he remebers that look from minutes ago and bites his tongue.

"And, don't ever bring it up – "

"I won't."

" – with anyone."

"I won't. It's okay."

"It is not okay, Harry." Bob shakes his head, lowering his gaze from his friend. "You have no idea."

"You're right. I don't."

"Just shut up, man." Bob's really had enough. "Listen, go get some sleep below. I'll take us back and wake you to go ashore. You're driving, so be alert."

"We're not going to stick around Fortune for the day?"

"Fuck no. Not now." Bob's fed up. "We'll load the trailer, grab some burgers, I'll speak with Pop, and then we hit the road."

"Dude, it's already been a crazy-long day, can't we – "

"No."

"Man, I didn't mean to walk in – "

"Drop it."

"There's nothing wrong with two men – "

"Fucking merde, Harry! I don't need to hear this right now."

"Are you still going to pay me?"

"You'll earn it by keeping quiet."

Harry backs off, backing up and sliding silently through the door to the stairs below. He finds his bunk, but it's not like he can sleep like this. Instead, he drafts a stand-up routine in his notebook as the ship bobs back to shore.

Mercanary decides to harvest a feast instead of a snack.

The Unanswered Riddle

As a non sequitur response to Alice, the Mad Hatter asks, "Why is a raven like a writing desk?" (Carroll 60).

What is your response?

What do you make of this unanswered riddle?

What purpose does it serve in this tale for children?

Carroll finally offers up an answer in 1896: "...what seems to me to be a fairly appropriate answer, viz., 'Because it can produce a few notes, though they are *very* flat, and it is *nevar* put with the wrong end in front'" (Carroll 6).

This strikes me as a coy response. It is almost as if Carroll wished to maintain the mystique of the unanswered riddle while appeasing those demanding an answer.

I imagine that Dodgson – being a mathematician and a logician with an interest in wordplay – would be someone that appreciates the subtle difference between *how* and *why*.

The answer he provides in 1896 satisfies the riddle best if the riddle asked "*How* is a raven like a writing desk?"

But, that is not the riddle's wording; the riddle asked *why*.

So, I speculate that Carroll (Dodgson) may have intended the riddle to provoke curiosity.

By asking why, Carroll frames the question as one looking for a cause, a reason why.

If that is the case, then one might ask about any two subjects, as if they are variables, and the riddle functions as a lesson about juxtaposition and association.

Q: Why is A like B?

A: Because you framed the question that way, which implies a similarity exists between the two.

As such, if there is merit in the notion that Carroll was trying to teach lessons to children in addition to entertaining them, then this becomes a sort of lesson about the importance of how a question is framed.

Even if one accepts Carroll's text to be purely nonsense for entertainment, arguing that the author had no such intent here, then this remains a fascinating riddle, and this interpretation remains a valid response, albeit an entirely unamusing one.

In Time

Executrix: 2096

EXT. NEIGHBOURHOOD – BEFORE WORK
OR SCHOOL

FADE IN: Camera views neighbourhood and
home. A sidewalk, crosswalk, and embankment are
necessary scenery leading to bus stop.

INT. HOME – BEFORE WORK OR SCHOOL

Toilet flushes. KYLE CONNER watches his turd
twirl down the bowl. FATHER at door as KYLE
begins brushing teeth.

FATHER

(concerned-n-chill)

Finished your book report yet?

KYLE

(brushing teeth)

I will.

FATHER

She only let you do it on that gamebook
because you're doing well. Still true?

KYLE

Of course!

FATHER

Alright. What was that book again?

KYLE

(stoked)

The Warlock of Firetop Mountain.

FATHER

Yeah. Does she know you have to throw the
dice?

KYLE

She will. I'll finish on the bus.

FATHER

Alright. I have to leave for work.

KYLE

(spits in sink)

Yep!

FATHER exits.

MOTHER

(shouts from porch)

Your book report is due today!

KYLE

(brushing teeth)

I know.

MOTHER

Don't stay home watching cartoons!

KYLE

I know.

MOTHER

Lock the door!

KYLE

I know.

MOTHER

We love you!

KYLE

I know!

MOTHER

(blows kiss loudly)

And don't be late! Your bus!

MOTHER exits. KYLE wipes mouth, bounds to

living room, camera pans across '80s items, and he inserts a tape into the VCR. He sits on couch, watches *G.I. Joe* "Worlds Without End, Part 1." He waits. Phone rings.

KYLE

(answering phone)

Hello! This is the Conner residence.

EXECUTRIX

(polite phone voice)

Hello. Yes. Mr. Conner, please.

KYLE

Dad and Mom just left for work. It's just me here now, but Mom says that's okay because my bus comes at 7:45. Maybe you can call later!

EXECUTRIX

What? No, I can't. Mr. Conner should be home. He indicated he'd be there then. The estate allotted money for a single temporal-call in this proviso.

KYLE

I'm sorry. Dad isn't here.

EXECUTRIX

This can't be right. So, Kyle Conner can't speak with me now?

KYLE

That's not Dad! I'm Kyle!

EXECUTRIX

What? No. You sound too young.

KYLE

I'm 10! I'll be 11 in October. That's why I'm big enough to wait on my own.

EXECUTRIX

10? You're listed here as being 20.

KYLE

Okay. But, I'm 10, my birthday is Halloween, and I'm going as Marty McFly because I already have a life preserver from fishing with Dad.

EXECUTRIX

Lovely, but something is wrong. What year is it when you are?

KYLE

It is 1985.

EXECUTRIX

It should be 1995. I input the wrong number –

KYLE

Okay, lady. Goodbye!

EXECUTRIX

No! Wait! Don't go!

KYLE

Mom says ignore wrong numbers.

EXECUTRIX

You're the Kyle Conner I am looking for. It's just not the right time.

KYLE

What time is it where you are?

EXECUTRIX

I'm in the future. It is 2096.

KYLE

This sounds like a joke. Are you playing tricks?

EXECUTRIX

No, sir. We're required by law to inform the estate when asked.

KYLE

Okay. I have to catch my bus soon.

EXECUTRIX

Please, Mr. Conner, there's no money assigned for me to make a second call, and I really need to keep this job. You'll have to do.

KYLE

Do what?

EXECUTRIX

Sir, I must inform you that you expire in 2094 –

KYLE

Expire?

EXECUTRIX

– and, at that time, you had no heirs to collect your wealth.

KYLE

My wealth?

EXECUTRIX

Yes, Mr. Conner. In 2042, you won the mega-lottery, amassing a fortune valued at over $8 billion.

KYLE

Wow!

EXECUTRIX

Yes, but you instructed the executors of your estate to get in touch with your younger self to ask how the remainder of your fortune should be distributed.

KYLE

I'm going to be rich?

EXECUTRIX

Yes, Mr. Conner. You will be richer than half
the world's population combined. That is certain.

KYLE

Wow.

EXECUTRIX

And, how should we divide your remaining
wealth, Mr. Conner?

KYLE

Feed the hungry? Mom says to eat my peas
'cause some kids have nothing.

EXECUTRIX

(joyful, relieved)

Thank you, Mr. Conner! You don't understand
how much that means to me, but thank you! That
is all I require. Have a fantastic day!

The call ends without any dial tone. KYLE is
baffled and in awe. He hangs up the receiver, stops
the tape (does not eject it), turns off the TV, grabs
his backpack, and runs out the door, forgetting to
lock it.

EXT. NEIGHBOURHOOD – BEFORE WORK
OR SCHOOL

KYLE exits his home and runs off to the bus stop.

230

He scurries down the embankment, gains momentum, and runs out onto the crosswalk without looking either way.

ABRUPT CUT TO BLACK. A deep horn honks as tires screech before there is a small thud. Bystanders are heard in shock and grief.

THE END

Swapped

Bob paid Harry in cash when they returned to town, but Harry hasn't heard from his friend since they parted ways. He's not even reading Harry's texts, given the lack of receipt. Marg's not replying, either.

Mercanary appreciates the ability to summon friends during such dark times.

Scarlett's out working another split shift, Max is drying her hair, spiking it, and Harry's slouched on the sofa, staring at the messages on his phone. He waits for a response he doesn't get.

Minutes pass and then Max darts down the stairs, across the living room, and into the kitchen.

"Harry?" she calls out, her head tucked inside the fridge.

"Yeah."

"Those reviews you've done – "

"Yeah?"

" – do we even have any mustard?"

"What?"

Mercanary approves of St. Vincent's manner of
moistly speaking.

"Never mind," she says, closing the fridge door
with mustard in-hand. "Listen. Those reviews
you've done, they're alright."

"Thanks."

"Hey!" she bellows. "What's up your arse this
afternoon?"

"What? No. Nothing. What's up?"

"Shit, Harry, I'm just trying to say your work is
decent, b'y."

"I appreciate it, Max. I try."

"I know you do," she assures him. "It shows.
You've got a real voice that comes through."

"Thanks, Max."

"Listen, Harry, I don't know what's got you so
sunk, but I'm trying to hook you up with another
opportunity here. Perk up, b'y."

"Gotcha! I'm here. Thanks to the max! What's
the story, chief?"

"SongzYaWanna."

"For real?"

"Lisa bailed. We need this coverage, and I'm all tied up." Max grins and adds, "Harry, you're our only hope."

>Mercanary appreciates that adventures in
>Wonderland may require a mask.

"This one pays, yeah?"

"Yeah. There's grant money for this hype story. I'll hook you up."

"I've never written anything like this before."

"Yeah, but you've read *Rolling Stone*. Just write some kind of gonzo piece of rock journalism. We want something real wild to print. You know. Just hype the bands and make the festival sound cool. I'll edit it before it goes to print. You'll be fine. You'll be better than fine; you'll rock, son!"

Mercanary listens to her pitch. It's sound. He looks to Harry eagerly.

>Mercanary appreciates there is a strange loop in
>both art and history.

"I'm on it."

"Fuck yeah!" Max is both thrilled and relieved. She didn't even have to leave the apartment to find a fix for this hitch. Then, she fixes herself a sandwich.

Mercanary unloads the magazines from his dual

assault rifles.

RA-TA-TA-TA-TA-TATATATATATAH!

The shells burst into confetti, and then Mercanary swims circles around Harry and Max.

Harry's stoked about this new opportunity. He returns to his dungeon to prepare. Instead, however, he writes short stories – fantasies mostly – with Mercanary by his side.

> Mercanary appreciates he'd never be here
> without a great debt to his roots.

Without a real job, Harry scribbles away the time with his fantasies until the festival begins that Friday night.

The bar is packed. Bodies press upon bodies on the dancefloor as the crowd shuffles with its own life in The Stone Hearth, a trendy venue with a second level overlooking the stage. No band is on yet. The show is already an hour past schedule, but no one cares. This is how it goes. The house DJ spins tracks as a prelude to the night's showcase. Beats rumble deep and steam rises from the crowd.

Harry slides in past the line at the door. He flashes a press pass and feels like a rock star. Mercanary's already inside. He dances through the air between levels as Harry takes in the scene, spotting Scarlett and Rei sharing drinks and laughs in a booth along the wall. He nods in their direction. They don't notice him. He sidles up to the bar, finding Vince as he orders a pair of cocktails.

Mercanary appreciates white rabbits lead to silly dreams. Mercanary also appreciates such nonsense.

"How's it go, Harry?"

"It goes well enough, I s'pose."

"That's never a bad way of looking at it."

"Perspective certainly helps. Isn't this the midterm break? Shouldn't you be grading essays or something?"

"Patti's playing."

"She is?"

"Yeah, Tanx Grrlz are opening."

"Holy shit! That's sick. How'd they get a gig like SongzYaWanna? Isn't this their first show?"

"Ha! No. They've played a few now, but they're filling in here tonight. Young Goodman Grue had to cancel."

"Jesus! That's the same reason I'm here."

"What?"

"I'm covering the festival for *The Overpass*."

"Really?"

"Yeah, man!"

"That's wild! I thought I heard Lisa Welles was working the festival this year."

"I dunno, Vince. I can tell ya she isn't, because I'm here."

"Who knows, right?"

"This is it. This is lit."

Mercanary appreciates you can be more than one thing – Veritech, Decepticon, Autobot, and Cobra. Mercanary also appreciates those who imagine a Veritech rather than seeing a Gundam here.

"Do they ever start on time at these shows?"

"No. You in a rush or something?"

"I told Patti I'd be here to see her perform, but I really have to get back to work."

"At this hour on a Friday night, you have to get back to work?"

"Yes."

"You really walk the walk, eh b'y?"

"I live it."

"Don't we all?"

"That's true," Vince replies as he's finally served. "Harry, I'm going to be away for a conference next week. Can I get you to substitute for my lectures?"

"What the fuck, Vince? I'm not a professor. I can't teach." To the bartender, Harry adds, "One tall absinthe."

"You don't have to teach them anything. I have notes prepared. You'd just have to present three hours of lectures. There's no real work besides babysitting my class while I'm away. Just be present."

"I don't know, Vince. It seems like a lot. I dunno. What if I freeze up?"

"They'll eat you alive. They prefer raw flesh."

"What?"

"They won't care. Even if it gets awkward, just roll with it."

"What do I know, Vince? They'll know I'm an imposter!"

"We're all fakes, Harry," Vince assures him. "I'll pay you $300 per lecture. If I hear it goes well, I'll tip you another hundred."

"You'll pay me a thousand bucks to babysit some students for, like, three hours next week?"

"Yeah. That's the sum of it."

"You got it!"

Mercanary appreciates one can virtually sail the seas of cheese.

The two shake hands to seal the deal, Vince

238

takes his cocktails upstairs, and Harry awaits his tall order of absinthe. It's served to him without ritual. He tips fairly without complaint and turns to size up the scene when Iggy and Jack Everhard pull up to the bar in a pincer's movement.

"Holy shit, b'ys!" Harry didn't think he'd see the Everhard's in town, and he'd never think they were into shows like this. "What are ye doin' here?"

"We needed a break from bay life," Iggy explains. "Jack and Nadine had some drama. We're here for the space."

"Fuck you, Iggy," Jack asserts. "It's not that bad. She'll be best kind after a few days."

"Yis."

"B'ys, I'm glad you're here," Harry admits as he steps away from the bar so the brothers can squeeze in to order drinks.

Mercanary appreciates werewolves of a variety of places.

The three joke and chat and catch up on the news quickly enough, but then Harry gets stuck the moment they tell him Rae's died.

What?

Yeah.

Seriously?

For real.

Up away in Alberta, she had an accident.

Some say it was an accident, but others say it was drugs.

Does it matter?

All Harry hears is Raelyn's dead.

It's like these phrases repeat.

Rae's died.

Rae's dead.

It was an accident.

It was drugs.

Rae's dead.

Rae's died.

It was an accident, regardless.

Harry and the Everhard's conversation continues, but Harry's mind has checked out altogether.

Time implodes.

They order more drinks.

They go outside and into the alley for a smoke.

They smoke two joints.

The brothers laugh, and Harry laughs along with them but his mind races through every memory of Raelyn that he had previously tried to erase. Harry's running on autopilot, but he's also running out of fuel.

Jack gives him a handful of magic.

Harry gulps it down with a swig.

The three go back inside to enjoy the show.

Harry's got to get to work.

A punk band rocks. Animal heads bop across the stage. A bear rattles the drumkit like a zoo's cage, a horse thrashes guitar riffs, a goat thumbs the bass, and an owl screeches into the mic. It's mayhem maybe.

Harry pushes the brothers into the pit, and then he drifts to the sidelines. He takes notes, jotting descriptions, but it's useless.

Rae's died.

He tears out a page, and tries again.

Rae's dead.

His thoughts race. Song after song, he's lost.

And then, reality **b l o o m S** .

Harry stuffs his notepad into his ass pocket, tucks his pen behind his ear, and slithers through the crowd.

Mercanary appreciates a good game as well as a good reading list.

He swears the goat is making eyes at him, but he pushes on to the stairs and climbs to the backstage greenroom where he finds the headliners, The Wizard's Tarot.

The doorway gives way to the chamber where the band chills.

Harry trips through the door.

They look up to him.

He asks, "Do you believe in rock'n'roll?"

"What?"

"This interview's over," Harry replies. Turning on his heel, he trips across the door's frame and stumbles back toward the stairs.

A goat greets him. Harry can't make out what's said, and then she lets out a whinny like a proper nanny.

Harry leans hard against the wall.

The goat comes closer. Her breasts press against Harry's chest. He can feel her heart beat when she bleats in his ear. Then, she slides her fingers inside his belt.

Harry doesn't resist.

The pair press against the wall and shimmy behind a curtain.

Rae's dead.

The goat undoes Harry's belt, letting his jeans drop to catch at his knees. Harry unzips the goat's fly. She unbuttons her shirt.

Rae's died.

Harry's hard up. She takes him in.

He pumps. She moistens.

He thrusts. She glides.

He kisses her breasts, he licks her collar, and then he brushes his lip up along the side of her neck, lifting the goat mask up as he goes.

Mercanary appreciates one's sections.

"Patti?" He's mid-thrust.

Patti moans, "Yes!"

"Patti! What the fuck?" He pumps again.

"Yes!"

"What? No." He withdraws.

"What the fuck, Harry?"

"No. I can't."

"Fuckin' fuck me!"

"I can't! What about Vince?"

"Vince left already. You're here with me. Now fuck me right already!"

"What? No. I thought you were an owl!"

243

"You're fucking useless, Harry." She pulls on her leggings, grabs her shirt closed, and pushes past Harry through the curtain, scorned and furious.

Harry's clueless. Fumbling to zip up, he plods down the stairs like it's some unholy rabbit hole. He walks across the dancefloor. He doesn't see Patti. He doesn't see Vince. He doesn't see Scarlett or Rei.

Rae's died.

Raelyn Poppy's dead, and he'll never have a chance to make things right.

Harry makes a dash for the door like a drunk about to puke, but, when the cool air hits him, he just lights up a smoke.

"Hey. I know you."

I'm a scholar
I enjoy scholarly pursuits

In Humour

Haaaaa... (big breath)

So, things and stuff,

am I right? **LOL**

Hashtag comedy.

Ughhh...

Don't worry. I

promise I'll be more

articulate than that.

I dunno if it'll be

funny, but wordy is
     guaranteed.

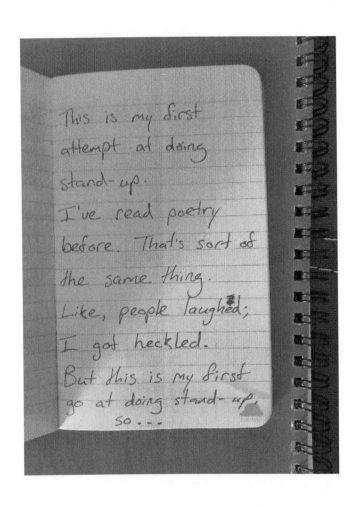

This is my first
attempt at doing
stand-up.
I've read poetry
before. That's sort of
the same thing.
Like, people laughed;
I got heckled.
But this is my first
go at doing stand-up,
so . . .

Everything's going to
be okay?
So, I'll tell you
right from the start:
I'm kind of cheating.
I chose a premise
that plays to my
strengths.
You see, I wrote
you these limericks.

(Take out 1 of 2
notebooks. _Dramatic._)
Oh, wait!
DISCLAIMER: For
the record, this
skit is entirely NON-
PARTISAN comedy,
none of which is
the truth, the whole
truth, nor anything

even resembling
the truth.

I had to say that.
Wait again! THAT
was the truth.

Are you familiar with
the Liar's Paradox?

Never mind.

It's all going to
be okay.

So, I wrote you
these limericks.
OH!. You see, I
chose this premise
so I could have
this prop.
I mean, it's not
just so I could
write these things
down and feel

like it's okay for
me to just straight
up read from it,
which — while
perhaps clever —
would be an
entirely valid criticism
of my whole act.
Have at it.
There it is.

Fair enough.

It's not even that
original, really.
I mean, it's totally
inspired by a bit by
Rik Mayall, but
I'm not exactly
ripping him off here
or anything.

Like, okay, sure,
he did read poetry
as a stand-up
routine. Granted.
Mine's legally distinct!
I swear.
Hahaaa. (Nervous breath)
RIP Rik Mayall.
Yeah.
Still.

Valid criticism.

I already said that.

Right?

But, _no_! It's not

JUST that.

It's also so I can

have this handy prop —

right here in my hand

even — providing me

something to wave

about wildly, like
a madman, <u>and</u>
to distract your eye.
(<u>Wave</u>. <u>Throw</u>. <u>Reveal</u>.)
Like, everyone's looking
at me, right? C'mon!
The book! Look at
the book! Okay,
sometimes. Sometimes
look at the book.

Gimme a break,

right?

I need a drink.

(Drink.)

Right.

So, I wrote you

these limericks.

Sorry? How am

I for time?

About 60 seconds?

Shit.

Okay. Uhhh...

Where was I again?

Right!

So, I wrote you

this limerick.

AHEM

One second.

AHEM

Educated

Harry wakes with the morning's light and with Rei pinning his left arm.

He jolts upright, clutching his arm to his neck.

She wakes. She smiles and rolls over, mumbling, "Shower's all yours."

"I – I can't remember last night."

"Ha! No. You wouldn't. It was magical!"

Harry finds himself in what could be her bedroom, her apartment? "Where are we?"

"My office."

"Your office is a loft?"

"Yes. At the gallery. On top."

Harry shifts a curtain to find a familiar view.

"Did we – "

"Did we fuck?"

"Yeah?"

"No."

Oh?

"Oh?"

"No. Came here. Real hot and steamy. I showered and shaved. You read me your notes."

"I did?"

Did he?

"You did," she says. "We cuddled. You weren't making any sense. We slept. Now you can shower and go."

"Yeah?"

"Don't push your luck. I'm not your mother."

"Shit. I didn't say you were."

"Fuck off. Lemme sleep."

Harry skips the shower and picks up his things. He takes the spiral staircase down past the studio full of nudes and down to the gallery's main floor. Mercanary's waiting for him at the door. He hands Harry a smoke and they walk from downtown to Neverland.

Writing this piece for *The Overpass* is a nightmare in itself. Harry can't recall anything besides speaking with Vince and the Everhards.

Rae's dead.

Rae died.

So much of it is a blank. His notes offer little to fill in the missing pieces. He writes a piece that indulges the spectacle of the show: the people, the crowd. He writes everything blurrily, as if seen through fogged glasses. He closes it with his interview of The Wizard's Tarot, and then he emails the article to Max. It's not fit.

He finds himself in the kitchen fixing up enough beans and rice to feed four for a week when Scarlett skips into the kitchen.

"Can I get at the stove? I just want to fry an egg."

"Yeah. I'll get out of your way. Just a sec."

Scarlett lets out an exaggerated whinny.

Harry doesn't remember, but he twitches at her goat impersonation.

"What's that for?"

"Tanx Grrlz! That nanny goat was a hottie." She mimics the goat's call again.

Harry shivers.

"You alright? Looks like you've just seen a ghost."

"Maybe I did. I'm hungover something wicked."

"Understood," Scarlett says. "I feel fucking

great!"

"That's great. Work's treatin' you well, eh?"

"Fuck work. I'm so sick of these split shifts. Forget about that. I mean... I think I'm in love."

"For real? Holy shit! I didn't even know you were seeing anyone?"

"Fuck off, Harry. Yes, you do."

"What? Who?"

"Rei. You met her here. It was at your party. We were all drinking absinthe and... "

Harry listens, but his mind is running multiple complex processes in order to compartmentalize his own reality into something he can cope with in the moment.

Mercanary appreciates the mystical powers of imagination yet acknowledges that, like any placebo, it can only accomplish so much.

He smiles and nods.

He says he's happy for her.

She's in her glee. She thinks Harry's just hungover.

Scarlett leaves for the first part of her shift.

Harry goes to work reviewing Vince's lecture notes for this coming week of substituting.

"Stick to the script, and everything will be just

263

fine," Mercanary assures Harry as they go down to read together in the dungeon.

Vince's notes are sparse, however, and much is assumed. Facts and concepts the professor would simply know off-hand are left out altogether, and Harry can't quite make the leap for each connection.

"This isn't much of a script, Mercanary."

Mercanary shrugs, but then he holds the text aloft: *The Tempest*.

"Just stick to the script, and everything will be fine."

Mercanary appreciates a good bedtime story at this hour.

It's never easy to rise on a Monday morning, and Harry's extra nervous about this gig. Off the books, this is just a favour for a friend, but Harry can't help but dream of what the professorly life must be like: reading endlessly, pursuing research interests, crafting rhetoric, disseminating knowledge, being salaried, having dignity, and the like.

Harry's dressed to play the role. He's done his hair and is brushing his teeth while Mercanary chases him all over the apartment wearing a cap and gown, scribbling notes on a parchment with one of his own quills. Grooming is important to make a good impression on the students, he writes.

Harry looks at himself in the mirror.

He breathes deeply, and then he leaves for class.

Finding the classroom on campus reminds Harry of being lost here himself as a first-year student. At the door, he asks Mercanary to wait out of sight so he won't be distracted by his awesomeness.

"I am that awesome. You're right!" Then the mythical beast-thing takes flight, zooming down the corridor and out the building's entrance.

Harry sets foot in the classroom to teach for the first time. He sorts through his notes at the podium beside the professor's desk. It's his desk now. It's his for a time, at least.

"Who are you, sir?"

"I'm Harrison Bueller. I'll be filling in for Dr. Lee this week."

"Awwww," some students moan as a chorus.

Do they miss Vince already?

"Where's Prof. Lee?" another student asks.

"He's away – " Harry makes eye contact with the speaker and recognizes the familiar face. It's Tyler from Copy Matters, that dude with a thing for Scarlett. Harry shakes the memory from his mind. Maybe the recognition's not mutual. He starts over, saying, "Dr. Lee is attending a conference this week, so I'm just here to keep things on track while he's away."

Mercanary appreciates the morning for its
poetic justice.

Harry's inexperienced, so he doesn't recall right
away how some students view substitutes.

What can they get away with now?

How far can they push him before he snaps?

"Now, I'm told you've been reading William
Shakespeare's *The Tempest*. If we follow Dr. Lee's
notes, then we should clue up Act IV by the end of
Wednesday. For Friday, we should be moving on
to begin Act V."

"Sir!" It's Tyler.

"Yes?"

"Prof. Lee always lets us read for the first 15
minutes of class each Monday."

"Does he?" Harry scans the other students for
reactions, but most remain uninterested and
apathetic, giving him no signs to read. He suspects
Tyler is full of shit.

"Yeah. He leaves us alone to read. I think he
goes out for a smoke."

"Is that so?"

"Well, I don't know what he's smoking, but – "

A few students beside Tyler chortle.

Tyler pauses for this predictable laugh track, and then he continues, saying, " – he really seems to enjoy it."

Harry eyes the lot of them, and then he quickly restrains his vicious glare.

There's a brief yet potent moment of silence in which Harry cracks the joints in his neck with the crick of his head and then, tight-lipped, he runs his tongue across the front of his teeth.

"Right," Harry resumes, regaining his composure. "Well, I think change can be a good thing, so we'll stick to the script, meaning I'm going to lead you through a discussion of Act IV today and Wednesday. Friday, we begin Act V."

Indeed, Harry presents the notes that Vince had prepared for him. The remainder of the lecture goes tolerably well. Tyler and his cronies are just a minor nuisance. However, after an hour's lecture, he's already through all of Vince's notes for Act IV. He notices this as he dismisses the class, and a sense of panic lies latent underneath his eerily calm façade.

Mercanary appreciates dada as well as what is now.

Mercanary dives into the classroom through a closed window, smashlessly, and then he shoots sparklers from his dual machine guns of celebration. Harry smiles, relieved that the window's not broken and the floor's not singed. Mercanary plops an apple onto the desk, beaming a brilliant smile at his friend. Harry takes a bite from it, and then the two return home to the dungeon to prepare something for the next class.

They're re-reading *The Tempest*, and each of the pair perform the parts. This is when Harry hears the front door open and slam closed.

"Harry?" It's Max.

"In here!"

Max stalks across the porch to his bedroom door. She kicks it open with her foot as she steps in to confront the author, printed pages in-hand. "What the fuck is this?"

"My article?"

"This is not an article."

"Yeah, it is."

"HARRY!"

"What?"

"We can't print this shit."

"Why not? What's wrong with it?"

"There's nothing in here about the festival!"

"There's plenty there about the festival. What do you mean?"

"What the fuck, Harry? There's nothing in here

268

about any of the performances from The Stone Hearth, and there's nothing about the bands even. What were you thinking?"

"You asked me to write something gonzo to hype the festival. That's what I did."

"What? How?"

"Like, I focused on the people. That's the story. It's a gonzo story, just like you requested."

"This isn't what we had in mind."

"This is a sensational piece! It'll be legendary!"

Mercanary appreciates how this may seem like a momentous event.

"It'd be infamous, Harry. I can't even cut this into something useful. There's nothing about Young Goodman Grue – "

"They didn't even show up!"

" – and there's nothing about Tanx Grrlz – "

Harry squirms and retorts, "That's fair. I didn't know they were playing, though."

" – and there's nothing about The Wizard's Tarot – "

"There is so!"

"That doesn't count."

"It should."

"I don't know how I'm going to fix this."

"I don't know what to tell ya, Max. I did the job you hired me to do."

"Harry," Max says with a sombre tone, "I can't pay you for this."

"What! Why not?"

"There's grant money funding our work on the festival. They wouldn't give us another dime if we ran this story."

"I did the assignment, chief."

"You didn't, Harry."

"Fuck that noise, Max. I could invent an entirely new artform – like, a memeoem or something – and not even that would be good enough to please you, would it?" Harry's pissed, but he's in the middle of trying to work another gig. "Look, I have to get back to this for Vince. He's paying me."

"Whatever. I have to get back to fixing your bullshit mess."

Max tosses the papers at Harry. They swirl apart and plummet to the floor. Harry doesn't bother picking them up. Instead, he returns his head to his book.

The two roommates avoid each other that evening and throughout Tuesday. Harry and Mercanary keep to themselves in the dungeon.

Mercanary practices shapeshifting, taking on the various forms of the characters that Harry's studying, summoning costumes and effects from the very æther. Nevertheless, Harry struggles to make sense of his life while reviewing the masque of Act IV. It's not easy.

Mercanary appreciates the bard as being both an artist and an entrepreneur. Mercanary also appreciates that the bard is the best player class.

Wednesday's lecture is derived from Harry's madness about the masque. He presents an interpretation of the text in contrast to what Vince had expressed in the notes.

"So, where Prof. Lee suggests that the masque is of little importance, I want you to see another side of the story here."

Tyler is challenging yet again, asking, "Is this going to be on the test?"

"What? I wouldn't know what your professor has in mind for your assignments. Wouldn't you have to write essays, anyway?"

"Test/essay. Whatever. Are we going to have to know this ever?"

"Ever? Someday, I s'pose. I can't say where your life might take you." Harry's getting saucy now.

"You know what I mean, sir. When are we ever

going to have to know anything about this play? Or Shakespeare? Or masques? It's not like literature matters."

"What the fuck?"

Ooops.

Some students gasp audibly. Oh, their innocent ears must be coddled more than this.

Mercanary appreciates the body of work that has come before as well as the rabbit holes yet to come.

"Sir – " Another student tries to step in with a comment. She fails.

"I can't believe you're a university student," Harry yells at Tyler, "and you have to ask if literature matters – "

"I didn't ask that," Tyler insists.

Harry raves on, shouting, "Literature most certainly matters. It matters to many. For fuck's sake, writing is almost time travel – "

"Is it now?" Tyler adds with a smirk.

"It most certainly is – now and always has been. This play was written over 400 years ago, we're reading it now, and the playwright's portrayal of this wild fantasy is still relevant today!"

"So what?"

"So? It means there's something human in it.

All literature is a voice, a human voice, and it can echo through time if the conditions are right."

"I think it's dated."

"Great! Just think something about the literature. You'll need to have thoughts about these things in order to write any essays." Harry's patience is lost. Exasperated, he goes on, explaining, "Shakespeare wrote this play late in his career, and you should recognize this as a work of allegorical metafiction. In a sense, the author of anything is the voice of every character they write. In prose, the author's the narrator, too. Now, this is a play, yes, but understand that Prospero is Shakespeare just as much as Shakespeare is Prospero. The Bard gets what it means to create a world, to give it life through words." Harry doesn't notice the few students rushing to jot down his rant; he just raves on. "That's part of what makes this masque so interesting. It was fairly trendy at the time to exploit the play-within-a-play technique. Oftentimes, this was to expose a villain's guilt, like in *Hamlet*. Here, however, the playwright's masque is utterly magical – it's a blessing – as Prospero performs his art. In the context of the play's narrative, the masque affirms Miranda and Ferdinand's innocent relationship. That's the surface of it. Underneath is where the magic can be found, and, in the context of an expression from the playwright, the masque demonstrates that nothing is beyond the power of the imagination when ink is put to paper. Listen: Campbell's sort of got the right idea in *The Hero with a Thousand Faces*, but if that's just the protagonist, then the author has a million more, surely."

Harry stops to catch his breath. He notices now that some students have their heads down, scribbling away, but he's still flustered. He dismisses the class 15 minutes early. Excusing himself, he's the first out the door as he's still stuffing his notes back into his satchel.

> Mercanary appreciates everyone's nerves are shot, but we can still be chill.

That evening at home, Harry rehearses Act V with Mercanary. Just going through the lines is all he can manage now. They stay up late. Max hasn't spoken more than three words to Harry since Monday's spat. Scarlett hasn't really been home much all week.

Harry wakes before noon the next day to the sound of voices out front.

It's Scarlett.

Rei's with her.

Harry stays in bed until he hears they've come inside and gone upstairs. After an hour, he goes upstairs to nuke some leftover rice and beans. He tosses the container into the microwave, hits the buttons thoughtlessly, and turns to find Rei and

Scarlett whispering in the dining room.

Shit, right? Like, if he had heard them there, he wouldn't have foraged for sustenance.

"Hey! I know you," Rei calls out to Harry.

Harry shudders.

"You sure do, Rei." Harry's façade is non-existent at this stage. Rei notices this, and she shoots him a look that says shut the fuck up.

> Mercanary appreciates one can have many layers.

Scarlett notices that brief look. Does she suspect something's up?

"Harry, what's going on with you and Max? The very air has turned to ice here this week."

"Ugh. Yeah. I know. It's tense."

"What's the drama then?" Rei asks.

Harry replies, "Money. Aesthetics. I dunno. Both of those, I guess."

"Shit," Scarlett says with sympathy. "You two get along so well! I'm sure you'll work this out."

"I'd have to get paid first."

"Ouch!" Rei adds, like she's watching a fight.

"This has to do with SongzYaWanna, right?"

"Yeah."

"I can't believe you two're in such a mess over that. We had a great time! Didn't we, Rei?"

"It was fun." Rei winks to Harry.

"I didn't even see you there. What happened to you that night, Harry?"

He doesn't answer. He hardly knows, but he remembers waking up with Rei. He's staring at her now. She waits for him to say something, anything. He doesn't. He still stares. Scarlett notices.

"Rei, did you see Harry at the show?"

"Only after."

"Oh?" Scarlett and Harry supply this synchronous reply.

"Harry was in a state after the show. I found him outside having a smoke. I brought him down to the office and laid out the couch for the drunk."

Mercanary appreciates artists with hustle and vision always, while also appreciating work clothes are for performing sometimes. Mercanary also appreciates the appropriate use of apostrophe in addition to grammatically effective apostrophes.

"Drunk?" Harry's ire is provoked by her diction. "I had a lot going on."

"Yeah, I'm sure you did," Rei retorts.

"Look, I don't know if we fucked or what – "

"What!" Rei and Scarlett respond together.

276

This is escalating quickly.

" – all I know is we woke, together, naked, and you had me pinned to the bed."

"What the fuck, Harry!" The pair of lovers speak as one again.

Rei looks to Harry, shooting daggers at his throat to cut out his tongue.

Scarlett looks to Rei, as if searching for the woman she loves.

Loved?

Who knows?

"Rei, what's going on?"

"I – I – I don't know why he's saying th– "

"Scarlett, Rei and I fucked."

"What!" Rei and Scarlett respond together, again.

"We didn't fuck after the show!"

"Not that night, we didn't."

"What the fuck, Rei! What's going on here?"

"I – I – "

"Scarlett, I'm sorry. You two have a lot to talk about, and I have to study for Friday's class." Harry's despondent, and he continues, stating, "I'm moving out."

Mercanary appreciates that the grind must go on.

He leaves the two lovers fighting. He returns to studying *The Tempest*. Mercanary sits behind Harry on the bed. With his downy soft wings, he gently plugs Harry's ears.

Harry doesn't get out of bed Friday morning. In his place, Mercanary delivers the lecture.

Leap of Fate: A Fable to Some

A scholar tutored an impatient prince, His Sovereign, after a prestigious career in educating the royals. Lessons took place in the palace, in the courtyard, and in the countryside often enough.

His Sovereign was destined to rule the land one day. Subjects assured His Sovereign of that fact nearly every time they spoke to His Sovereign.

The scholar took great joy in attempting to educate His Sovereign, as his was a position of influence, affording him many comforts and luxuries, like soft pillows and sugary cakes.

His Sovereign was still young, however, boisterous and naive, unlike His Sovergein's elder sister, the princess, Her Dame. Her Dame was a marvelous pupil, courteous yet keen. Her Dame so charmed the scholar that he often overestimated His Sovereign's intellect.

His Sovereign's ultimate lesson occured alongside the bleak precipice of a deep ravine. The scholar, using stones and sticks, was etching figures in the dirt, rambling about pies and Pythagoras, but His Sovereign was distracted, wondering about trajectories instead.

His Sovereign spied a willow tree that clutched the edge of the cliff from which, His Sovereign supposed, one could swing across the ravine, escaping a boring lecture to adventure where the scholar dare not follow.

The scholar reminded His Sovereign that there was a chance of crashing upon the distant rocks below, and that that was a risk worth some caution.

His Sovereign asked the scholar how there could be any risk when His Sovereign was destined to rule. The scholar replied that, given the circumstances and the context, each of us must decide our own fate, and he was pleased His Sovereign appeared to be learning.

His Sovereign did not follow, however. All anyone has ever said to His Sovereign reinforced his conviction. His Sovereign was destined to rule the land, and His Sovereign thought that that must include the willow, the ravine, and the pastures beyond. A single scholar's single lesson would not be accepted by His Sovereign. It was simply disagreeable.

So, His Sovereign reprimanded the scholar's impudence, and he leapt out to the willow's overreaching branch.

Of course, His Sovereign's grasp was too slack, and His Sovereign plummeted to a bloody demise.

The scholar was distraught but still quite aloof. Upon reporting the untimely demise of His Sovereign he remarked that it was an unfortunate leap of fate, a joke at which only he laughed.

The scholar was sentenced to death for his untimely attempt at humour.

Some years passed, and Her Dame later ruled the land, and the subjects were well satisfied.

THE END

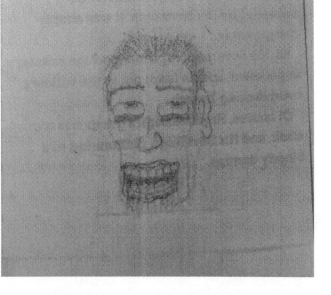

Blessed

Harry gets out of bed Saturday afternoon, waking from a bad dream. He's ususally ignorant of his dreams, but this one haunts his consciousness. The grotesque Troll-Cat of his imaginings had placed him in bondage, torturing him throughout an eternity of dream-time. It leaves Harry feeling hollow. He tries to shake it off. Checking his phone, he does a triple take upon seeing the date and time.

"Shit, shit, shit, shit, shit! What the fuck happened?"

Mercanary shrugs with a sly grin.

"Brrreeep!" says Harry's phone.

He sees an email notification from Vince.

"Dude, this can't be good. I slept through Friday's class. Shit. Vince's going to be fuming!"

He taps the alert and reads:

Harry,

Thanks for covering my lectures this week!

Kayla – my brightest pupil – already messaged me through Farcebark to express how brilliant you were filling in for me. She said yesterday's lecture was really something else, entirely unbelievable even!

I don't know how you managed it; she's a tough critic to please, I know.

I'll see you soon, dude!

Thanks again!

Vince

Harry looks to Mercanary in disbelief, and he asks, "How can this be?"

Mercanary appreciates St. Vincent's quarantine shopping mood.

"I saw how stressed out you were, so I let you sleep in," Mercanary answers. "I substituted for you, just like you did for Vincent."

"You did what?"

But Harry's phone speaks up before Mercanary could go on, adding, "Brrreeep! Brrreeep!"

A text from Rei is followed by another from Scarlett.

He checks Rei's first.

Thanks, asshole. You ruined a good thing.

> *I'm sorry, Rei. Maybe we could have had something nice. I didn't know you and Scarlett were so serious.*

You think I mean us? HAHAHAHAHAHA!

> *Yeah. I mean, we had something hot.*

We had a fling! You're just one cock like all the rest. You fucked up. Scarlett is done with me. I'm totally done with you.

> *You never told me there were others!*

Done. Over. Quit texting me. Don't even wave in my direction, cuck.

Harry doesn't respond. Let it be done.

What's next?

Harry checks the message from Scarlett, who's probably just up on the third, but whatever.

When are you moving out?

ASAP. Gotta find a place first.

I'm keeping your deposit because of this.

Good enough.

Well, that's that.

Mercanary follows Harry up to the kitchen where they re-fry another helping of rice and beans. They hear music coming from the third. Scarlett's playing Arcade Fire's *Funeral*.

They return to the dungeon to eat their lunch, and Harry finds another text waiting on his phone. It's from Max.

Publisher says we have to pay you for the job. Grant reporting and such. Not printing your story. I re-wrote the article. Byline: Overpass Staff.

Thanks, Max.

We're printing your reviews. Keep the books.
Byline: Overpass Staff.

WTF! Can't I get credit for those?

Publisher says we'll pay you for that botched gig,
but we don't have to endorse you. Ever.

Wow. Thanks.

And then, that's that.

Harry wonders what might have happened to Bob. He checks Immedia, but Bob hasn't posted anything in a couple of weeks. He checks Bob's Farcebark profile. Still, no new posts in weeks. Then, Harry notices Bob's relationship status is set as single.

"Fuck," he says to Mercanary.

"I don't know, man. Look to see if they're still friends."

He searches Bob's list of connections, but Marg

isn't even listed.

"What's even going on this year, Mercanary?"

"I can't say. It beats me."

"Is this my fault?"

"What? No, man! How could this have anything to do with you?"

"Bob's fucked off since I caught him with his pants down."

"Right. Yes. Okay."

"I don't see how that could lead to this?"

"Neither do I."

Sometimes, what appears to be non sequitur to the observer is merely a causal chain with unseen links.

They don't get it. It's personal, but it's between Bob and Marg and the horse.

Harry messages Bob, checking in.

Consuming his meagre sustenance, he just stares at his phone, again waiting to hear back from his friend.

"Brrreeep!"

Harry hits the notification before looking.

It's another email from Vince.

Harry,

Just checked my work emails, and there is a shitstorm of complaints – from my students and my superiors – about Friday's class.

This isn't good.

My tenure track could be in jeopardy because of this.

What the fuck happened in Friday's class?

Get back to me with answers.

Vince

Harry looks to Mercanary pleadingly, and asks, "What happened in yesterday's class?"

Mercanary appreciates clear messaging in self-portraiture.

"I covered for you!"

"What do you mean, though? How? What did you do?"

"I stuck to the script, just like we had practiced, and I read through Act V and the Epilogue. That's about it."

"Are you sure?"

"Totally! The students were captivated by my performance!"

"I don't know about that."

Mercanary appreciates the power of a good dream.

Harry emails his response to Vince.

I don't even know what happened Friday.

I've sort of been in the depths of a shitstorm, and the shit winds have been blowin' a fierce gale.

I just don't know.

Harry

About 15 minutes later, Vince sends his reply.

This isn't good.

I'll transfer you $900. No tip.

I'll need time to deal with this. I'll get in touch if I need you.

Vince

Not knowing any better, Harry supposes that's fair enough.

He leaves his lunch half-finished and absentmindedly dawdles with packing and throwing out old junk.

Mercanary takes out the trash and finds a loathsome feral cat stalking the street. They eye each other with suspicion before Mercanary returns to his friend.

> Mercanary appreciates we are all cooped up gazing out the rear window these days.

"Mercanary, what am I going to do?"

"To be or Bartle-be – that is the real question, Harry. I know you'll survive!"

"How? I'm jobless again, and now I dunno if I even have any friends left in this town!"

"I'm still here."

"Yeah, but what the fuck are you?"

"I'm your friend, Harry!"

Harry regards himself in his dresser's mirror, and he replies, "Really? What good is that?"

Mercanary looks hurt.

He's never looked so sad, but it doesn't linger long before his smile returns and his beak is fully agape with the purest joy.

Mercanary wraps his downy wings around Harry, squatting him lovingly from behind. The two reflect upon their nature in the mirror for what feels like forever.

And then, without speaking another word, Mercanary releases Harry, he steps back from him, he bows graciously to his friend, and he leaves.

Mercanary appreciates characters that exhibit growth.

Harry watches the beast-thing walk through his bedroom door, and then he hears the front entrance open and close.

He doesn't see Mercanary and the Troll-Cat outside of his dungeon on the street.

He doesn't see these two figments as their gazes meet and they walk down into town.

Alone, Harry keeps sorting through his mess, searching for something bright to cling onto. Instead, his spirits sink. He finds an ad online for a basement bachelor's apartment, and he agrees to sign the lease without viewing the place. He's fine with that. It helps to keep moving, and he decides to hire some help moving his things.

Mercanary and the Troll-Cat follow the same path through the capital, keeping an eye on one another from opposite sides of each street along the way. They're like this down Thorburn to Freshwater, from Freshwater to Merrymeeting, and then from Merrymeeting, crossing streets and eight-way intersections, all the way down to Harbour Drive and until they reach the Terry Fox monument beside the harbour. They are locked onto each other the entire time.

Harry calls each of his sisters overseas and then

he phones his parents in Harbour Grace. He lets each of them know that he's having a rough time, but he only provides them with limited details. It's too much to explain, but he gives them an honest account of the gist of it: a series of unfortunate misunderstandings has led to deeply problematic personal conflicts, so now he has to move.

His sisters send their love and offer to help from afar however they can.

His parents reassure him that he can always come home to stay no matter what the trouble may be.

Harry appreciates their support, but he knows he needs to fix this himself.

Troll-Cat wades into the harbour, taunting Mercanary to follow.

Mercanary empties dual magazines into the sky, and then he charges his nemesis, yelling, "COO, COOOOOO!"

Mercanary appreciates empathy more than masochism, but it is what it is.

They clash like unnatural forces, sending an explosion of blinding light throughout the city and ringing thunder that sounds across the Atlantic.

No one in St. John's notices the ill-conceived weather.

No one at Neverland is speaking to Harry, so he

avoids his roommates throughout the week and takes his meals to the dungeon. With the hired help, Harry's cleared out of Neverland as quickly as practical.

Troll-Cat and Mercanary fight viciously with no holds barred, but the fiend maintains control over the flow of this conflict. Furiously, he holds Mercanary's head beneath the surface of the seawater.

Alone in his new place, Harry's spirits sink further the more time that passes without hearing from his friends. Then, he cracks, texting each of them his apologies.

Troll-Cat pulls Mercanary's head up only to thrust it back underwater, over and over and again and again. Mercanary gasps for air each time despite knowing he can breathe underwater.

Dusk turns to night turns to dawn, and Harry still hasn't heard from his friends. So much is left un-unpacked. The storm rages on outside.

The Troll-Cat's grown in size. He's a tremendous kaiju now, mucking about in the harbour beneath the moonlit silhouette of Cabot Tower on Signal Hill. Stomping Mercanary's broken body into the harbour's floor, Troll-Cat supplements each stomp with a grinding twist. The foul demon trills a sickening purr that rumbles along with the accompanying thunder. The beating continues throughout the night.

Harry's plagued with nightmares still, and he's noticing them all now. He hasn't noticed his own nightmares since he was a young boy. He's concerned, asking himself, What's he supposed to do now? Where's he supposed to go? Should he enlist?

Troll-Cat releases Mercanary from underfoot only to gloat to his face with that shrill, gargling purr of his, a sadistic look in his eye.

These troubles aren't new to Harry, no, but this time he has an epiphany.

Mercanary's gaze meets Troll-Cat's, but something has changed.

Now, he is unafraid.

Mercanary appreciates the subtle nuances of pronouns.

He thinks to himself, No! I've made some mistakes, but I've tried to do alright.

Although the water's rough and he's been beaten down, Mercanary stands.

Harry's picking up his trash, and he thinks, I'm only human. I know I've made some mistakes – a lot of them, actually – and that's my own fault.

Troll-Cat steps upon his head, but Mercanary holds his massive claw aloft, and then he steps aside, letting it splash harmlessly into the water.

I'm just going to have to do my own thing. I

know I can't please everyone all the time. I need to focus on pleasing myself, but I need to make amends somehow.

Mercanary looks defiantly into the face of the kaiju Troll-Cat.

No one wants to hear from me. Okay. There's nothing I can do about that. For my part, I still want to express my apologies, though. How? How can I do that if they won't listen?

Mercanary's regaining his strength. Harry's demons are the wind beneath his wings, and he's rising to confront the archfiend itself.

I know! I'll write each of them letters. Everyone I've hurt, I know where they live, so I can mail my apologies to them!

Mercanary takes flight like a rocket aimed at the Troll-Cat's fearsome maw. He strikes with more force than he's ever mustered, yet Troll-Cat only squirms and then snorts a little laugh. He's hardly fazed by the blow.

But, like, they might not even read it if I send them letters. They might just toss them into the trash with the rest of the junk mail.

Troll-Cat swipes Mercanary away from his face like some pesky mosquito. The villain absorbs such woe and transforms again, taking on aspects of many fearful creatures. It's as if he's becoming the omni-terror, a thing far worse than any

Antichrist or Cthulhu.

Harry asks himself, What else can I do?

Troll-Cat laughs triumphantly at Mercanary, who seems lost having delivered such a powerful blow that resulted in no meaningful impact.

That's when Harry remembers when he first met the mercanary, and then – as he's dropping off his garbage at the curb – it hits him.

A sparkle glistens suddenly in Mercanary's eyes.

I know! I'll write a book!

The storm breaks, and a ray of sun pierces through the clouds to enlighten Harry.

Mercanary floats in the air. As he tilts his head upward, he closes his eyes and stretches his wings outward, welcoming.

I'll write a book to apologize! It can be like Plato's *Apology*, and I'll write this book, and it will be a testament to my apologies whether they read it or not!

The sun shines upon them all now.

Mercanary basks in the full rays of the sun, and it's as if all things pure and good the world over lend him strength.

Harry gets straight to writing apology letters until he falls asleep at his desk.

Mercanary battles Troll-Cat. It's an epic clash of titans in the harbour. When night falls, they fight on until morning.

Harry awakes the next morning with a mission and a new sense of purpose, and he leaves for the post before getting a coffee.

Mercanary and Troll-Cat continue to trade blows, but when Harry purchases stamps from the vending machine, Mercanary lands a solid strike with each coin spent. Troll-Cat is rocked, but he's not down yet.

Harry licks and fastens each of four stamps to each of four envelopes containing genuine apologies.

Mercanary appreciates each of the 36 chambers, like an art.

Mercanary connects with a four-blow combination. Troll-Cat stumbles back, and Mercanary flies up into the sky. He breaks through the upper atmosphere and drinks up the sun's light, powering up from these cosmic energies.

And, when Harry lets the four letters fall into the mailbox as one pile, Mercanary crashes down onto the staggered Troll-Cat, producing such an impactful blast – like nothing ever imagined prior – that it reduces the dreaded thing to his petty, frail form, that of a sickly little sphynx.

Mercanary appreciates revelations as well as

revolutions.

Harry stops into the convenience store before returning home to finish packing. He wanted another pack of smokes, but he only asks the clerk for a sparkling water.

The clerk asks, "You don't need a ticket to go with that?"

"What?"

"The lottery, b'y! Grand prize's over ten million."

"Is that right? Nah, I'm good. Just the water. Thanks."

"You sure? You've got to be in it to win it, ya know."

"Oh, I know. No worries."

"Okay. Your loss, buddy. That'll be a buck sixty-five."

"Eh, b'y. Wait. I'll take a pack of those Semi-Sweet Rosebuds, too."

The clerk rings it in. "Four-twenty."

> Mercanary appreciates there are many games through which one gains.

Outside, Harry opens the bottle, takes a swig, retrieves his phone, and dials a familiar number.

"Hello?"

"Hi, Mom. I'm sorry I've given you so much grief. I'd like to come out for a visit. Is that cool?"

"Yes, my son! You knows you can come visit! Your father might not say it, but he'll be some pleased to see you. Will you be staying with us long? All that trouble you mentioned and all, I mean."

"No. I just want to see you and Dad. It's okay. I'm doing well despite it all now, I think."

"If you say so."

"Yeah. It'll be okay. I'll drive out this afternoon if that works for ye."

"Yeeesss, my dear!"

"Perfect. I'll see you then. Much love to you both!"

"HA! Yes, now! Much love, I'm sure."

"It's true."

"If you say so."

"You'll see. I'll be out in a couple of hours. Cheers!"

"Bye, bye!"

Harry sits behind the wheel, opens the box, fills his palm with semi-sweets, and then stuffs them in his mouth, savouring each endorphin released.

Mercanary floats over the defeated Troll-Cat.

300

He extends his wing.

A paw accepts a helping hand.

Harry's placing his phone back into his pocket when a gentle gust blows a piece of paper right through the car's window and into his mouth.

"Pah-tooh," Harry spits. "What the fuck is this garbage?"

He grabs the slip, opens it, and finds that it's a lotto ticket.

Taking Troll-Cat by the paw, Mercanary smiles upon Harry from afar. Comforted now, knowing that everything's going to be okay, the two sail away between the peaks of the Narrows toward the limitless horizon and into the sun's light.

MERCANARY
A Zine of Poetry and Adventure

Words and images by David Reynolds
© April 2019

For more official Problematic Press
publications, follow us on:
Facebook @ProblematicPress
Instagram @problematicpress
Or just problematicpress.com

AUTHOR'S NOTE

In the sincerest voice of the author, I wish to thank my family and friends for their love and support. I'd never have reached this opportunity in life without you. Thank you dearly. I appreciate it.

This novel is the result of an experiment, which attempts to adapt a 'zine of poetry and adventure by first adapting the 'zine into a memeoem that would then act as the basis for writing the rough draft of this novel.

A memeoem is a collage sequence that uses Instagram stories as its medium. While I doubt I invented this new poetic art form, I may have coined the term. Naturally, a sells-word would.

The Epic and Labours of the MERCANARY™ can be found @the.mercanary, but be aware it is already degrading. It's only ephemera, after all.

The curious may crave the following list of selected allusions. Please, read and enjoy!

ALLUSIONS

Aesop. *Aesop's Fables*. Translated by V.S. Vernon Jones, illustrated by Arthur Rackham, Wordsworth Classics, 1994.

---. "The Crow and the Pitcher." *Vester Vade Mecum: A Collection of Short Fiction*, illustrated and edited by David Reynolds, Problematic Press, 2013, p. 9.

Aesop Rock. *Spirit World Field Guide*, Rhymesayers Entertainment, 2020. *Spotify*, open.spotify.com/playlist/6B6uyzV5DkZwx RdFP1nqxx

AmaLee. "Life Will Change (from *Persona 5*)." *Total Coverage, Vol. 4*, Leegion Creative, 2018. *Spotify*, open.spotify.com/playlist/0aIQXlLqTH8U8p WD8TVD1D

Anamanaguchi. "Mermaid." *Dawn Metropolis*, Polyvinyl Record Co., 2009. *Spotify*, open.spotify.com/playlist/0aIQXlLqTH8U8p

WD8TVD1D

Anchor Zone. Directed by Andrée Pelletier, Red Ochre Productions, 1994.

Antwoord, Die. "Enter the Ninja." *O*, Die Antwoord, 2010. *Spotify*, open.spotify.com/playlist/0aIQXlLqTH8U8p WD8TVD1D

Arcade Fire. "Rococo." *The Suburbs*, Merge Records, 2010. *Spotify*, open.spotify.com/playlist/0aIQXlLqTH8U8p WD8TVD1D

Atwood, Margaret. "Happy Endings." *Literature: A Portable Anthology*, 3rd ed., edited by Janet E. Gardner et al., Bedford/St. Martin's, 2013, pp. 326-329.

---. *The Penelopiad*. Vintage Canada, 2006.

Austin, J.L. *How To Do Things With Words*. 2nd ed., edited by J.O. Urmson and Marina Sbisà, Harvard University Press, 1975.

BA Johnston. "Dayoff Is a Dayoff." *Gremlins 3*, Wyatt, 2017. *Spotify*, open.spotify.com/playlist/0aIQXlLqTH8U8p WD8TVD1D

---. "We're All Going to Jail (Except Pete, He's Going to Die)." *The Skid is Hot Tonight*, Transistor 66, 2018. *Spotify*, open.spotify.com/playlist/0aIQXlLqTH8U8p

WD8TVD1D

Band Ladies. "Not 24." *Angry All the Time*,
  Band Ladies, 2020. *Spotify*,
  open.spotify.com/playlist/0aIQXlLqTH8U8p
  WD8TVD1D

Barrie, J.M. *Peter Pan*. Random House, 1992.

Barthes, Roland. *Mythologies*. Translated by
  Annette Lavers, Hill and Wang, 1972.

---. *The Pleasure of the Text*. Translated by
  Richard Miller, Hill and Wang, 1975.

---. *Writing Degree Zero*. Translated by Annette
  Lavers and Colin Smith, prefaced by Susan
  Sontag, Hill and Wang, 1977.

Beastie Boys. "Gratitude." *Check Your Head*,
  Capitol Records, 1992. *Spotify*,
  open.spotify.com/playlist/0aIQXlLqTH8U8p
  WD8TVD1D

Beck. "Motherfucker." *Mellow Gold*, DGC
  Records, 1994. *Spotify*,
  open.spotify.com/playlist/0aIQXlLqTH8U8p
  WD8TVD1D

Beethoven, Ludwig van, Igor Levit, Cologne
  Chamber Orchestra, and Helmut Muller-
  Bruhl. "Piano Concerto No. 1 in C Major,
  Op. 15: I, Allegro con brio." *Beethoven:
  Piano Concertos Nos 1-5*, Naxos, 2007.
  Spotify,

open.spotify.com/playlist/0aIQXlLqTH8U8p
WD8TVD1D

Belle and Sebastian. "Get me Away from Here,
I'm Dying." *If You're Feeling Sinister*,
Jeepster Records, 1996. *Spotify*,
open.spotify.com/playlist/0aIQXlLqTH8U8p
WD8TVD1D

Bellows, Henry Adams, trans. *The Poetic Edda:
The Mythological Poems*. Dover
Publications, 2004.

Benson, Jodi. "Part of Your World." *The Little
Mermaid*, Walt Disney Records, 1989.
Spotify,
open.spotify.com/playlist/0aIQXlLqTH8U8p
WD8TVD1D

Björk. "Big Time Sensuality." *Debut*, Elektra
Entertainment, 1993. *Spotify*,
open.spotify.com/playlist/0aIQXlLqTH8U8p
WD8TVD1D

---. "It's Oh So Quiet." *Post*, Elektra
Entertainment, 1995. *Spotify*,
open.spotify.com/playlist/0aIQXlLqTH8U8p
WD8TVD1D

Black Market Hard-Tack. "Made Right Here."
Black Market Hard-Tack, Black Market
Hard-Tack, 2018. *Spotify*, open.spotify.com/
playlist/0aIQXlLqTH8U8pWD8TVD1D

---. "Ten Cent Plague." *Mass for Shut-Ins*,

Black Market Hard-Tack, 2017. *Spotify*, open.spotify.com/playlist/0aIQXlLqTH8U8p WD8TVD1D

Blake, William. "A Poison Tree." *Literature: A Portable Anthology*, 3rd ed., edited by Janet E. Gardner et al., Bedford/St. Martin's, 2013, p. 475.

Blondie. "Dreaming." *Eat to the Beat*, Chrysalis Records, 1979. *Spotify*, open.spotify.com/playlist/0aIQXlLqTH8U8p WD8TVD1D

Bulmahn, Jason. *Pathfinder Core Rulebook*, 1st ed. Paizo Publishing, 2009.

Byock, Jesse, trans. *Sagas and Myths of the Northmen*. Penguin Epics, 2006.

Campbell, Joseph. *The Hero's Journey*. Directed by Janelle Balnicke and David Kennard, William Free Productions, 1987.

---. *The Hero with a Thousand Faces*, 2nd ed. Princeton University Press, 1968.

Camus, Albert. *The Myth of Sisyphus*. Translated by Justin O'Brien, Penguin Books, 2005.

Carpenter, John Allan, BBC Concert Orchestra, and Keith Lockhart. "Enter the 'Mysterious Stranger'." *Carpenter: Krazy Kat*, Dutton Epoch, 2015. *Spotify*,

open.spotify.com/playlist/0aIQXlLqTH8U8p
WD8TVD1D

Carroll, Lewis. *Alice's Adventures in Wonderland and Through the Looking-Glass*. Edited by Peter Hunt, illustrated by John Tenniel, Oxford University Press, 2009.

Cat Empire, The. "Hello." *The Cat Empire*, Virgin Records, 2003. *Spotify*, open.spotify.com/playlist/0aIQXlLqTH8U8p WD8TVD1D

Chemical Brothers, The. "Free Yourself." *No Geography*, Virgin EMI Records, 2019. *Spotify*, open.spotify.com/playlist/0aIQXlLqTH8U8p WD8TVD1D

Chingon. "Malagueña Salerosa." *Mexican Spaghetti Western*, Rocket Racing Rebels, 2004. *Spotify*, open.spotify.com/playlist/0aIQXlLqTH8U8p WD8TVD1D

Cline, Ernest. *Ready Player One*. Broadway Books, 2015.

Cobley, Paul, and Litza Jansz. *Introducing: Semiotics*. Edited by Richard Appignanesi, Totem Books, 2007.

Confucius. *The Analects*. Translated by William Edward Soothill, edited by Thomas Crofts, Dover Publications, 1995.

Cypress Hill. "Hits from the Bong." *Black Sunday*, Ruffhouse, 1993. *Spotify*, open.spotify.com/playlist/0aIQXlLqTH8U8p WD8TVD1D

Dallas, Ian. *What Remains of Edith Finch*. Playstation 4 version, Annapurna Interactive, 2017.

DANGERDOOM. "Basket Case." *The Mouse and the Mask*, Epitaph Records, 2005. *Spotify*, open.spotify.com/playlist/0aIQXlLqTH8U8p WD8TVD1D

Deltron 3030. "3030." *Deltron 3030*, 75Ark, 2000. *Spotify*, open.spotify.com/playlist/0aIQXlLqTH8U8p WD8TVD1D

---. "National Movie Review." *Deltron 3030*, 75Ark, 2000. *Spotify*, open.spotify.com/playlist/0aIQXlLqTH8U8p WD8TVD1D

Dethklok. "Detharmonic." *The Dethalbum*, Williams Street, 2007. *Spotify*, open.spotify.com/playlist/0aIQXlLqTH8U8p WD8TVD1D

---. "Murmaider." *The Dethalbum*, Williams Street, 2007. *Spotify*, open.spotify.com/playlist/0aIQXlLqTH8U8p WD8TVD1D

Doors, The. "People Are Strange." *Strange Days*, Elektra Records, 1967. *Spotify*, open.spotify.com/playlist/0aIQXlLqTH8U8pWD8TVD1D

Elevator to Hell. "Roger and the Hair." *Parts 1-3*, Sub Pop, 1996. *Spotify*, open.spotify.com/playlist/0aIQXlLqTH8U8pWD8TVD1D

Elvis Costello and the Attractions. "Everyday I Write the Book." *Punch the Clock*, Columbia, 1983. *Spotify*, open.spotify.com/playlist/0aIQXlLqTH8U8pWD8TVD1D

Flaming Lips, The. "Yoshimi Battles the Pink Robots, Pt. 1." *Yoshimi Battles the Pink Robots*, Warner Bros., 2002. *Spotify*, open.spotify.com/playlist/0aIQXlLqTH8U8pWD8TVD1D

Flock of Seagulls, A. "I Ran (So Far Away)." *A Flock of Seagulls*, Jive, 1982. *Spotify*, open.spotify.com/playlist/0aIQXlLqTH8U8pWD8TVD1D

Franz Ferdinand. "Take Me Out." *Franz Ferdinand*, Domino Recording Company, 2003. *Spotify*, open.spotify.com/playlist/0aIQXlLqTH8U8pWD8TVD1D

Fugees. "The Mask." *The Score*, Ruffhouse, 1996. *Spotify*,

open.spotify.com/playlist/0aIQXlLqTH8U8p
WD8TVD1D

Garbage, and Nellee Hooper. "#1 Crush."
*William Shakespeare's Romeo + Juliet:
Music from the Motion Picture*, Capitol,
1996. *Spotify*,
open.spotify.com/playlist/0aIQXlLqTH8U8p
WD8TVD1D

Gogol Bordello. "60 Revolutions." *Gypsy
Punks: Underdog World Strike*,
SideOneDummy Records, 2005. *Spotify*,
open.spotify.com/playlist/0aIQXlLqTH8U8p
WD8TVD1D

---. "Wanderlust King." *Live From Axis Mundi*,
SideOneDummy Records, 2009. *Spotify*,
open.spotify.com/playlist/0aIQXlLqTH8U8p
WD8TVD1D

Golden Orchestra, The. "Superman Theme."
Superman: The Origins of a Superhero,
Golden Records, 2014. *Spotify*,
open.spotify.com/playlist/0aIQXlLqTH8U8p
WD8TVD1D

Golding, William. *Lord of the Flies*. Faber and
Faber, 1958.

Goldman, Emma. *Anarchism and Other Essays*.
Dover Publications, 1969.

---. *Mother Earth*, vol. 1., no. 1, Emma
Goldman, 1906.

---. *The Social Significance of the Modern Drama*. The Copp Clark Company, 1914.

Goodman, Nelson. *Fact, Fiction, & Forecast*. Harvard University Press, 1955.

Gorillaz. "Rhinestone Eyes." *Plastic Beach*, Parlophone, 2010. *Spotify*, open.spotify.com/playlist/0aIQXlLqTH8U8pWD8TVD1D

---. "Tomorrow Comes Today." *Gorillaz*, Parlophone, 2001. *Spotify*, open.spotify.com/playlist/0aIQXlLqTH8U8pWD8TVD1D

Great Big Sea. "Excursion Around the Bay." *Great Big Sea*, NRA Productions, 1993. *Spotify*, open.spotify.com/playlist/0aIQXlLqTH8U8pWD8TVD1D

Green Day. "All By Myself." *Dookie*, Reprise Records, 1994. *Spotify*, open.spotify.com/playlist/0aIQXlLqTH8U8pWD8TVD1D

Grouplove. "Back in the '90s." *BoJack Horseman*, Lakeshore Records, 2017. *Spotify*, open.spotify.com/playlist/0aIQXlLqTH8U8pWD8TVD1D

Hama, Larry. "Snake-Eyes: The Origin." *G.I. Joe Comics Magazine*, vol. 1, no. 10, Marvel Comics, 1988.

---. "Snake-Eyes: The Origin, Part II." *G.I. Joe Comics Magazine*, vol. 1, no. 10, Marvel Comics, 1988.

Hashino, Katsura. *Persona 5*. Playstation 4 version, Atlus USA, 2017.

Hawthorne, Nathaniel. "Young Goodman Brown." *Vester Vade Mecum: A Collection of Short Fiction*, edited by David Reynolds, Problematic Press, 2013, pp. 65-73.

Hemingway, Ernest. "Hills Like White Elephants." *Literature: A Portable Anthology*, 3rd ed., edited by Janet E. Gardner et al., Bedford/St. Martin's, 2013, pp. 212-216.

Hisaishi, Joe, and London Symphony Orchestra. "Kiki's Delivery Service." *Melodyphony*, Universal Music, 2010. *Spotify*, open.spotify.com/playlist/0aIQXlLqTH8U8p WD8TVD1D

Homer. *The Odyssey*. Translated by George Herbert Palmer, Dover Publications, 1999.

It Could Be Franky. "Sleep the Clock Around." *We All Know How This Will End*, Insert Name Here Productions, 2019. *Spotify*, open.spotify.com/playlist/0aIQXlLqTH8U8p WD8TVD1D

Iwatani, Toru. *Pac-Man*. Midway Mini Arcade

version, Coleco, 1981.

Jackson, Shirley. "The Lottery." *Literature: A Portable Anthology*, 3rd ed., edited by Janet E. Gardner et al., Bedford/St. Martin's, 2013, pp. 242-249.

Jackson, Steve, and Ian Livingstone. *The Warlock of Firetop Mountain*. Illustrated by Russ Nicholson, Puffin Books, 1982.

Jean, Wyclef, and Refugee All Stars. "Apocalypse." *Wyclef Jean Presents The Carnival*, Columbia Records, 1997. *Spotify*, open.spotify.com/playlist/0aIQXlLqTH8U8p WD8TVD1D

Jefferson Airplane. "White Rabbit." *Surrealistic Pillow*, RCA Victor, 1967. *Spotify*, open.spotify.com/playlist/0aIQXlLqTH8U8p WD8TVD1D

K, Joe. *Being or Nothingness*. Joe K, 2007.

Kripke, Saul A. *Naming and Necessity*. Harvard University Press, 1980.

Le Tigre. "Slideshow At Free University." *Le Tigre*, Mr. Lady Records, 1999. *Spotify*, open.spotify.com/playlist/0aIQXlLqTH8U8p WD8TVD1D

LL Cool J. "I'm That Type Of Guy." *Walking with a Panther*, Def Jam, 1989. *Spotify*, open.spotify.com/playlist/0aIQXlLqTH8U8p

WD8TVD1D

London Music Works. "Mighty Mouse."
Mighty Mouse, Silva Screen Records, 2014.
Spotify,
open.spotify.com/playlist/0aIQXlLqTH8U8p
WD8TVD1D

Lovecraft, H.P. *The Call of Cthulhu and Other Weird Stories*. Edited by S.T. Joshi, Penguin Classics, 1999.

Mack, Craig. "Flava in Ya Ear." *Project: Funk da World*, Bad Boy Records, 1994. *Spotify*,
open.spotify.com/playlist/0aIQXlLqTH8U8p
WD8TVD1D

Madonna. "Human Nature." *Bedtime Stories*, Maverick, 1994. *Spotify*,
open.spotify.com/playlist/0aIQXlLqTH8U8p
WD8TVD1D

Mankiewicz, Herman J., and Orson Welles.
Citizen Kane. Mercury Productions, 1941.

McLuhan, Marshall. *Understanding Media: The Extensions of Man*. McGraw-Hill, 1965.

McLuhan, Marshall, and Quentin Fiore. *The Medium Is the Massage: An Inventory of Effects*. Bantam Books, 1967.

Melville, Herman. "Bartleby, the Scrivener: A Story of Wall-Street." *Vester Vade Mecum: A Collection of Short Fiction*, edited by David

Reynolds, Problematic Press, 2013, pp. 105-129.

Metric. "Black Sheep." *Scott Pilgrim vs. The World*, ABKCO, 2010. *Spotify*, open.spotify.com/playlist/0aIQXlLqTH8U8p WD8TVD1D

MF DOOM. *BORN LIKE THIS*, Lex Records, 2009. *Spotify*, open.spotify.com/album/5i7JM6qlMK5x2gY 6Tkv56h

Miku and Friends. "Voices (from *Macross0*." *Happy Happy (Japan Anime Special)*, Cyber Chord Records, 2011.

Missy Elliott. "Work It." *Under Construction*, The Goldmind, 2002. *Spotify*, open.spotify.com/playlist/0aIQXlLqTH8U8p WD8TVD1D

Miyamoto, Musashi. *The Book of Five Rings*. Translated by Thomas Cleary, Shambala Publications, 2005.

Moby. "James Bond Theme." *I Like to Score*, Elektra, 1997. *Spotify*, open.spotify.com/playlist/0aIQXlLqTH8U8p WD8TVD1D

Monty Python. "Always Look on the Bright Side of Life." *Monty Python Sings*, Virgin Records, 1989. *Spotify*, open.spotify.com/playlist/0aIQXlLqTH8U8p

WD8TVD1D

Morine, Nicholas. *Steel Sarcophagus*. Brass Castle Books, 2020.

Nas. "I Can." *God's Son*, Ill Will, 2002. *Spotify*, open.spotify.com/playlist/0aIQXlLqTH8U8p WD8TVD1D

Negativland. "This Is Not Normal." *True False*, Seeland, 2019. *Spotify*, open.spotify.com/playlist/0aIQXlLqTH8U8p WD8TVD1D

Negativland, Chumbawamba, and DJ Dr. J. Land. "C Is for Stupid – ABCs Remix." *The ABCs of Anarchism*, Seeland, 1999. *Spotify*, open.spotify.com/playlist/0aIQXlLqTH8U8p WD8TVD1D

Neutral Milk Hotel. "Ghost." *In the Aeroplane Over the Sea*, Merge Records, 1998. *Spotify*, open.spotify.com/playlist/0aIQXlLqTH8U8p WD8TVD1D

Nine Inch Nails. "The Perfect Drug." *Lost Highway*, Nothing, 1997. *Spotify*, open.spotify.com/playlist/0aIQXlLqTH8U8p WD8TVD1D

NOFX. "Bob." *White Trash, Two Heebs, and a Bean*, Epitaph Records, 1992. *Spotify*, open.spotify.com/playlist/0aIQXlLqTH8U8p WD8TVD1D

---. "The Decline." *The Decline*, Fat Wreck Chords, 1999. *Spotify*, open.spotify.com/playlist/0aIQXlLqTH8U8p WD8TVD1D

Ono, Yoko. "Kiss Kiss Kiss." *Double Fantasy*, Geffen, 1980. *Spotify*, open.spotify.com/playlist/0aIQXlLqTH8U8p WD8TVD1D

Ono, Yoko, and Peaches. "Kiss Kiss Kiss." *Yes, I'm a Witch*, Astralworks, 2007. *Spotify*, open.spotify.com/playlist/0aIQXlLqTH8U8p WD8TVD1D

Operation Ivy. "Room Without a Window." *Operation Ivy (2007 remaster)*, Hellcat Records, 2007. *Spotify*, open.spotify.com/playlist/0aIQXlLqTH8U8p WD8TVD1D

Patti Smith Group. "Privilege (Set Me Free)." *Easter*, Arista, 1978. *Spotify*, open.spotify.com/playlist/0aIQXlLqTH8U8p WD8TVD1D

Pavement. "Cut Your Hair." *Crooked Rain, Crooked Rain*, Matador Records, 1994. *Spotify*, open.spotify.com/playlist/0aIQXlLqTH8U8p WD8TVD1D

Plato. *The Collected Dialogues*. Edited by Edith Hamilton and Huntington Cairns, translated by Lane Cooper et al., Princeton University Press, 2005.

---. *The Symposium*. Translated by Christopher Gill, Penguin Classics, 1999.

Poe, Edgar Allan. *The Fall of the House of Usher and Other Writings*. Edited by David Galloway, Penguin Classics, 1986.

Primus. "Jerry Was a Race Car Driver." *Sailing the Seas of Cheese*, Interscope, 1991. *Spotify*, open.spotify.com/playlist/0aIQXlLqTH8U8p WD8TVD1D

Public Enemy, and Stephen Stills. "He Got Game." *He Got Game*, Def Jam, 1998. *Spotify*, open.spotify.com/playlist/0aIQXlLqTH8U8p WD8TVD1D

PUP. "DVP." *The Dream Is Over*, Royal Mountain Records, 2016. *Spotify*, open.spotify.com/playlist/0aIQXlLqTH8U8p WD8TVD1D

---. "See You At Your Funeral." *Morbid Stuff*, Rise Records, 2019. *Spotify*, open.spotify.com/playlist/0aIQXlLqTH8U8p WD8TVD1D

Queen. "Another One Bites the Dust." *The Game*, EMI, 1980. *Spotify*, open.spotify.com/ playlist/0aIQXlLqTH8U8pWD8TVD1D

---. "Friends Will Be Friends." *A Kind of Magic*, EMI, 1986. *Spotify*, open.spotify.com/playlist/0aIQXlLqTH8U8p WD8TVD1D

Ramones. "Blitzkrieg Bop." *Ramones*, Sire Records, 1976. *Spotify*, open.spotify.com/playlist/0aIQXlLqTH8U8p WD8TVD1D

Reynolds, David. "BOAT TOURS! TEN BUCKS!" *The Cuffer Anthology*, vol. VII, edited by Pam Frampton, Killick Press, 2015, pp. 87-90.

---. *MERCANARY™ A 'Zine of Poetry and Adventure*. Problematic Press, 2019.

---. "Sabaku, the Deserter." *Late Night Dungeons*, vol. 1, edited by Nicholas Morine, Smashwords, 2011.

---. "The True Story of the Three Billy Goats Gruff: The Troll's Side of the Story." *Chalkdust & Chewing Gum*, Jesperson Press, 1992, p. 44.

Saban, Haim, and Shuki Levy. "He-Man and the Masters of the Universe." *He-Man and the Masters of the Universe*, CBS Records, 1984. *Spotify*, open.spotify.com/playlist/0aIQXlLqTH8U8p WD8TVD1D

Sato, Hiroaki, trans. *Legends of the Samurai*.

Konecky & Konecky, 1995.

Schiller, Friedrich. *On the Aesthetic Education of Man.* Translated by Reginald Snell, Dover Publications, 2004.

Shadowy Men on a Shadowy Planet. "Having an Average Weekend." *Savvy Show Stoppers*, Glass Records, 1988. *Spotify*, open.spotify.com/playlist/0aIQXlLqTH8U8p WD8TVD1D

Shakespeare, William. *The Tempest.* Edited by David Bevington, Bantam Books, 1988.

Simpsons, The. "Deep, Deep Trouble." *The Simpsons Sing the Blues*, Geffen Records, 1990. *Spotify*, open.spotify.com/playlist/0aIQXlLqTH8U8p WD8TVD1D

Slick Rick. "Children's Story." *The Great Adventures of Slick Rick*, Def Jam, 1988. *Spotify*, open.spotify.com/playlist/0aIQXlLqTH8U8p WD8TVD1D

SNFU. "G.I. Joe Gets Angry With Humankind." *Better Than a Stick in the Eye*, Cargo Records, 1988. *Spotify*, open.spotify.com/playlist/0aIQXlLqTH8U8p WD8TVD1D

Streets, The. "Stay Positive." *Original Pirate Material*, Locked On, 2002. *Spotify*,

open.spotify.com/playlist/0aIQXlLqTH8U8p
WD8TVD1D

St. Vincent. "Actor Out of Work." Ac*tor*, 4AD,
2009. *Spotify*,
open.spotify.com/playlist/0aIQXlLqTH8U8p
WD8TVD1D

---. "And Then She Kissed Me." *Universal
Love: Wedding Songs Reimagined*, Legacy
Recordings, 2018. *Spotify*, open.spotify.com/
playlist/0aIQXlLqTH8U8pWD8TVD1D

---. "Digital Witness." *St. Vincent*, Republic
Records, 2014. *Spotify*,
open.spotify.com/playlist/0aIQXlLqTH8U8p
WD8TVD1D

Sun-tzu. *The Art of War*. Translated by John
Minford, Penguin Books, 2005.

Thompson, Hunter S. *Fear and Loathing in Las
Vegas*. Illustrated by Ralph Steadman,
Vintage Books, 1998.

---. "The Kentucky Derby Is Decadent and
Depraved." *The Great Shark Hunt: Strange
Tales from a Strange Time*, Simon &
Schuster, 2003, pp. 24-38.

---. *The Rum Diary*. Simon & Schuster, 1998.

Toole, John Kennedy. *A Confederacy of
Dunces*. Grove Press, 1980.

Tragically Hip, The. "Poets." *Phantom Power*,

Universal, 1998. *Spotify*,
open.spotify.com/playlist/0aIQXlLqTH8U8p
WD8TVD1D

War. "Why Can't We Be Friends?" *Why Can't
We Be Friends?*, United Artists, 1975.
Spotify,
open.spotify.com/playlist/0aIQXlLqTH8U8p
WD8TVD1D

Waxman, Franz. "Rear Window Main Title."
Rear Window, Paramount Pictures, 1954.
Spotify,
open.spotify.com/playlist/0aIQXlLqTH8U8p
WD8TVD1D

Welles, Orson. *The Other Side of the Wind*.
Americas Film Conservancy, 2018.

Welsh, Irvine. *Trainspotting*. Minerva, 1997.

Wilde, Oscar. "The Happy Prince." *Vester Vade
Mecum: A Collection of Short Fiction*, edited
by David Reynolds, Problematic Press, 2013,
pp. 165-170.

Williams, John, and the London Symphony
Orchestra. "Princess Leia's Theme." *Star
Wars: A New Hope*, 20th Century, 1977.
Spotify,
open.spotify.com/playlist/0aIQXlLqTH8U8p
WD8TVD1D

Wittgenstein, Ludwig. *Philosophical
Investigations*. 3rd ed., translated by G.E.M.

Anscombe, Blackwell Publishing, 2005.

Wu-Tang Clan. "C.R.E.A.M." *Enter the Wu-Tang (36 Chambers)*, Loud Records, 1993. *Spotify*, open.spotify.com/playlist/0aIQXlLqTH8U8p WD8TVD1D

Yankovic, "Weird Al." "I Think I'm a Clone Now." *Permanent Record: Al in the Box*, Scotti Brothers Records, 1994. *Spotify*, open.spotify.com/playlist/0aIQXlLqTH8U8p WD8TVD1D

Zevon, Warren. "Werewolves of London." *A Quiet Normal Life: The Best of Warren Zevon*, Elektra, 1986. *Spotify*, open.spotify.com/playlist/0aIQXlLqTH8U8p WD8TVD1D

Žižek, Slavoj. *Event*. Penguin Books, 2014.

The End.

Find more Problematic Press content online at the following:

problematicpress.com

problematicpress.threadless.com

Instagrams

@the.mercanary

@problematicpress

@davaflavaprime